# Richard's Magic Book

By Elaine C.R. Heckingbottom

To Anna, Megan and Lucy

I know you're too old for it now, but you were amongst the first to read it originally, and I did promise!

As Nilbog says, 'A promise is a promise, you know!'

Also to Rachael, Elyse and Luke and the new generation; Tommy, Phoebe and Oliver.
Your mothers enjoyed it – I hope you will too!

# Chapter 1  <u>Why Me?</u>

Richard was eight and a half years old and, like a lot of other boys and girls of his age, he just wasn't interested in reading. It wasn't that he couldn't read. In fact, he could read quite well when he wanted to. The main problem was that there were so many more interesting things that he could have been doing:- playing football, watching television, building things with his Lego set, playing on the computer or with his Gameboy, or just playing with his friends. In fact, almost anything was preferable to reading. Reading just got in the way; and some of the books were so dull! Nothing much happened in them, and when it did, it was so unbelievable! They were always about children with funny names - Biff, Chip and Kipper for example, or Roger Red-Hat and Billy Blue-Hat. They were never about children with nice, normal names like his own; until, that is, the day his teacher handed him a brand new book.

"I got this especially for you, Richard," Mr James had said as he gave it to him. "As soon as I saw the title, I thought of you. I just had to get it; it had your name on it!" And when Richard looked at the title, he realised that his teacher was right. It DID have his name on it - in big letters, all over the front cover!

Richard's
Magic Book

by N. C. Lever-Clogs

"You might find it a bit hard to start with," Mr James had added, "but keep going and I'm sure you'll find it's worth it!" He winked at Richard. "It's a special one!"
"Thanks, Sir," Richard had replied - but he hadn't really meant it. This book was much thicker than the ones he normally picked up - over 60 pages -

and it had <u>chapters!</u>  Oh no!  At 5 or 6 pages a day (his normal rate) it would take him **forever** to read!  "Oh crumbs!" he thought to himself.  "It's not fair!  Why couldn't it have Amy's name on it - or Peter's?  At least they liked reading!  Why couldn't it have anyone else's name but mine?"  He shoved it into the bottom of his backpack, ready to take home.  "I bet it's really dull as well!" he muttered under his breath.  "Books always are!"

It wasn't until much later that night that Richard began to realise that this book might actually be rather different from anything he had ever read before.  Just before bedtime, his mother called to him to come and read, and so reluctantly, he opened it and began reading the first few sentences slowly and carefully to his mother.

## Chapter 1

Richard was like a lot of other boys and girls of his age. He just wasn't interested in reading. It wasn't that he couldn't read (although it was sometimes a bit hard to put the letters together to make a proper word!)
The main problem was that there were so many more interesting things that he could have been doing:- playing football, watching television, building things with his Lego set, playing with his computer or his Gameboy, even playing with his friends, anything! Reading just got in the way, and some of the books were so dull! Nothing much happened in them, and when it did, it was so unbelievable!
They were always about children with funny names - Biff, Chip and Kipper for example, or Roger Red-Hat and Billy Blue-Hat. They were never about children with nice, normal names like his own.

"Hey!" Richard said to his Mum, "This book really could be about me! That's how I feel every night!"
"It certainly could!" his mother replied. She was fed up with all the battles to try and get Richard to read a few pages of his book each night, and was

longing for him to begin to want to read for himself. Slowly and carefully they continued reading the next two pages together, then he turned over again and was astounded to see that he had read the first chapter already. It had been a lot shorter than he had feared!

"You see, Richard! You can do it!" his mother said, happily. "It's not that hard really!"

"I suppose not," Richard replied, as he put his book back into his book bag and went upstairs to bed. He was still thinking about what he had just read. The child in the book seemed to be so much like him, it was amazing! "I wonder......." he thought to himself. "But no - it couldn't possibly be......"

## Chapter 2   But What If?

Richard couldn't help wondering.  All that night he wondered - and much of the next day as well - so much so that he could hardly concentrate on his work!  What if the book really <u>was</u> about him?  What if it really <u>was</u> magic?  What might it be able to do?  Where might it be able to take him?  Richard had read all sorts of things about magic.  He had watched all the Harry Potter films - both in the cinema and on video - lots of times!  He had read the Magic Key books (He had no choice but to read them!  Everybody read them in his school, and he had to admit, they weren't all that bad!  At least they were more exciting than some of the things he'd had to read!)  He had quite enjoyed the story of The Magic Finger - his teacher had read it with them last year; and he'd wondered what it might be like to have magical powers (don't we all?  I know I do!) but he had dismissed it.  Surely there was no such thing as magic - and books couldn't possibly be magic ... could they?  That night, Richard couldn't wait to read a bit more of his book - just in case!  After all, you never know!  It might be magic - *really* magic - and there was only one way to find out.  As soon as he got into the house, he ran straight into the kitchen - but not to demand something to eat as he normally did.  This time, he wanted something quite different - and very surprising to anyone who knew him well.

"Mum, can I read some of my book to you?" he shouted as he ran into the house.

"Hang on a minute, Richard.  I'm rather busy right now." said Mum, not turning round.  She was mashing the potatoes to go on top of a shepherd's pie.  Suddenly, she realised what he had said and paused from what she was doing, looking round at him in surprise.
"Just a minute!  What was that?" she asked.  "What did you just say, Richard?  I can't have heard that right, - can I?"
"Can I read some of my new book with you?  Will you help me with it?"
"What, now?"

"Yes, now!  Please Mum!"

"But you haven't had your snack yet.  You're always starving when you get in from school.  And don't you want to watch your usual television programmes first?  I'm trying to get the tea on here!"

"Just five minutes, Mum - pleeeeease!" Richard pleaded.  Mum sat down next to him "Oh, all right then.  But I really can only spare five minutes right now.  I need to get this shepherd's pie in the oven, and there are lots of other things that need doing right now.  This place is a mess, and your Dad'll be home soon!  If you want to read any more than that, you'll have to read it to yourself - or read it to me later."

"OK," Richard replied - but as he opened the book and started to read the second chapter, he was in for his own second surprise.

### Chapter 2

Richard did wonder.  All that night he wondered - and much of the next day as well.  What if the book really <u>was</u>

about him?  What if it really <u>was</u> magic?
What might it be able to do?  Where
might it be able to take him?
Richard had read all sorts of things
about magic.  He had watched all the
Harry Potter films so far - both in the
cinema and on video - lots of times.
He had read the Magic Key books (He
had no choice but to read them!)  He
had heard the story of The Magic
Finger - his teacher had read it to them
last year.  He had thought about what
it might be like to have magical powers
(don't we all?) but he had dismissed it.
Surely there was no such thing as
magic - and books couldn't possibly be
magic ......... could they?


Richard was beginning to realise that there was

something rather special about this particular

book.  It was almost as if it could read his mind!

But surely no book could do that?

# Chapter 3    Nilbog ... and Adventure!

Slowly, Richard wandered upstairs to his bedroom, but he didn't switch on the T.V. - not yet.  He had far too much to think about right now.  He was convinced - he really DID have a magic book! After all, if it could read his thoughts, what else might it be able to do?

All the times he'd been made to read about the magic adventures of Biff, Chip, Kipper and Floppy with their magic key.  All the times when he'd tried to think about what he would do if HE had a Magic Key, and now, perhaps, he had that chance. It was almost too good to hope - but perhaps his turn had come!

He went over to his desk and grabbed a piece of paper and a pencil.  If HE were writing a magic book with magic adventures, where would he go first? What would he do?

Perhaps he could go watch United win the cup - but what if they lost?  It wouldn't be such a great adventure then, would it?

Perhaps he could go up in a rocket into space - or down in a submarine below the sea.

Perhaps he could fly to a mysterious island that no-one else had ever visited.

There were so many things to choose from. It was just too much for his brain to think about! He lay down on the bed and closed his eyes to try and think.

Suddenly, he heard something calling his name softly. He opened his eyes - and there in front of him was a small, elf-like creature with large, sticking out ears, a green beard and a funny, green Santa Claus type hat. Richard blinked. Hard. What was going on? Was he dreaming?

"Richard!"

"Who are you? What are you doing in my room?"

"I'm Nilbog. I'm the source of the magic in the book - your book."

"B... b... but I haven't read about you yet!" Richard stammered. "Where have you come from?"

"From your book! Look – I'm on the front cover! Surely you've spotted me there already?" Richard glanced down at the cover of the book. To his astonishment, Nilbog was right! The cover of the book had changed and there was now a simple portrait of someone who looked just like Nilbog! "You'll read more about me tonight or tomorrow," Nilbog promised, "when you read about your first adventure. Now, are you ready for it?"

"F... f .... first adventure? What do you mean?"

"Your first magical adventure. The owner of this book - you - the person who for whom it is being written - gets to go with me on five, special, magical adventures. The first one is ready and waiting for you, so are you going to stand there all evening with your mouth open, or are we going?"

"Err, I guess we're going!" Richard managed to reply, although he was still feeling rather flabbergasted. He couldn't quite believe his eyes - or his ears for that matter! "But where exactly? And how? And for how long?"

"Questions, questions, questions! All these questions! Asking questions never got anything done. Stop thinking, hold onto my coat tails, and off we go!  As for where - well, you'll see that when we get there, won't you!"

"But … Mum!  What will she think if I go missing?"

"We'll be back before she knows we've gone! That's magic for you!  Come on - you only live once!"

Still, Richard hesitated - but only briefly.  He knew all about Stranger Danger - but this was magic - it was real magic from his special book – the one that his teacher had given him.  It had to be safe! "OK Nilbog.  If you're sure we're safe, I'm ready," he announced, grabbing hold of the small elf's coat tails.  Let's go!"

## Chapter 4   Flying North!

Before Richard had time to think, they had flown straight out of the open window and were up and away; flying through the clouds like birds.  It was amazing!  He was higher than he'd ever been.  He looked down below, and saw his house disappearing into the distance, but somehow he wasn't afraid.  He didn't even feel cold, which surprised him!

"Where are we going, Nilbog?" asked Richard.

"Wait and see!" replied Nilbog, mysteriously.

"That's what Mum and Dad always say!" Richard grumbled.  "It's not fair!"

"Do you want to go home then?" Nilbog threatened.

"NO!" shouted Richard, "That's not what I meant at all.  I just wanted to know where we were going!"

"You'll find out when you get there!  Just sit back and enjoy it!  Look at all the things you can see."

"They always say that too!" Richard retorted, but he **did** start looking, and Nilbog was right - it **was** an amazing sight!  Peering down through the fluffy, cotton wool clouds, he could see the patchwork blanket of fields below. The cows and sheep seemed so tiny; they looked no bigger than the ones on his toy farm at home. He saw the river meandering through its valley on its journey to the sea, like a silky, silvery-grey snake, twisting and turning its way along its path.

They swooped down to weave their way, twisting and turning through a forest of trees. A couple of deer and their fawns paused nervously from their grazing in a clearing to look up and watch them pass. Next, they soared up, high into the sky to fly with the eagles, swooping and gliding over hills and mountains. "This is amazing, Nilbog!" Richard gasped. They flew over towns and villages, over streets and houses. Looking down, he could see what looked like small toy cars speeding along a toy road, and trains no bigger than those on his grandfather's model railway charging along their tracks. They flew further and further, and before long they reached the coast, where waves were crashing fiercely onto the rocks. On and on they flew, over sailboats and cruise-ships, past schools of spurting whales and leaping dolphins; further and further north all the time.

Suddenly they swooped down through a cloud of swirling snowflakes. Richard stuck out his tongue to catch one of them.  It gave him a delicious, tingly feeling all over!  He caught another and another, enjoying their feeling on his tongue, then as they swooped lower, down, down, down through the clouds.  He couldn't help himself – he had to look!   Just below them was a sparkling city of icebergs, some towering up almost like skyscrapers, others quite low.  Richard giggled as he spotted a polar bear sitting on the ice.
"Do you see that polar bear, Nilbog?" he laughed.
"Do you think his bottom will be cold?"
"Do you want to ask him?" suggested Nilbog.
"How could we?" Richard asked.  "I don't know how to speak Polar Bear!  I can't even speak French properly!"
"You do know how," replied Nilbog.  "Remember, this is a Magic Adventure.  Anything can happen

in magic adventures if we believe it!  That's magic for you!"

"But Polar Bears are fierce, aren't they?" Richard asked, nervously, looking at the huge creature that was perched on the ice below.

"Not this one!  He's just eaten!"

"What did he eat?"

"Ask him and see!" the elf replied.  They swooped down towards the iceberg and landed very close to where the Polar Bear was sitting.

"Hello, Nilbog!" the polar bear remarked.  "Who's this that you've brought along with you?"

"This is Richard," replied Nilbog, as Richard stood there with his mouth wide open.  "Richard - meet my friend Ralop."

"Your friend.....?"  Richard was astounded.  "You mean you know him?"

"Of course I do.  Do you think I would let you talk to strange animals?  That would be dangerous!  Now - didn't you have some questions to ask Ralop?"

"Well, yes, I did - sort of."

"Go on then.  What was it you wanted to know?" Ralop asked.

"Well, there were a few things really.  Mum always says I'm a bit like a walking question mark, 'cos. I'm always asking a lot of questions, but Dad says 'if you don't ask, you'll never know!'"

"Your Dad's right!  So go on then, and ask!" Ralop responded.

"OK, thanks!" Richard smiled, and asked his first question - the one he'd been dying to ask, ever since he's first seen Ralop!

"Don't you get a cold bum from sitting on icebergs all day long?"

"No - not really.  If you came and feel my fur, you'll see why." Richard did, and was really surprised.  Ralop's fur was not soft and fluffy, as he had expected.  It actually felt quite rough and greasy!  "All Polar Bears have thick, oily coats to protect them from the cold, and an extra layer of fat to help keep them warm; so we don't really feel the cold - even on our bottoms!" Ralop told him.

"How cold is it here?" asked Richard, adding another question to his list already.

"It can get as cold as minus thirty degrees centigrade - that's thirty degrees colder than it needs to be for water to freeze; but it's not quite as cold as that today!" Ralop replied.

"Crikey! That's really cold!" Richard shivered at the thought of it. He'd been doing some work on the weather in Geography at school, and they'd been recording the temperature every day for a while. He knew that thirty degrees above freezing was about the right temperature on a really hot, summer's day, but he'd not seen the temperature drop much below about -4° C, even when it had snowed in the middle of winter. Thirty degrees below freezing had to be bitterly cold! He was amazed to realise that he still didn't feel chilly at all! In fact, he was still quite warm! "Nilbog, why don't I feel cold right now if it's as cold as that here?"

Nilbog gave what Richard was soon to realise was one of his usual replies. "That's magic for you!"

he said. "Now, hurry up. We only have a few more minutes, and I know you have more things that you want to ask Ralop."

"Yes, I do. Nilbog said you had just eaten, Ralop. What do you eat?"

"All sorts of things," Ralop replied. "I'm a carnivore, so I just eat meat. Sometimes I'll eat a bird or two, and seals can be quite tasty too, but I don't usually eat humans - they're far too sweet tasting - especially children - so you're quite safe!" Richard was sure he winked at him! "Anyway, I've had a nice meal of fish an hour or so ago, so I'm not hungry any more. It was delicious!"

"How do you catch them?" asked Richard.

"Fish I have to go swimming for, but seals are easy. I wait at their breathing hole, and when one comes up for air, I catch it. All it takes is a bit of patience!"

"You really eat seals? Yuck - that's nasty!" Richard shuddered.

"No worse than you. You eat meat, don't you?" Nilbog added.

"Err, yes - I suppose I do." Richard replied

"Just because hamburgers and sausages don't arrive covered in fur and looking cute, you think it's different?"

"I suppose it isn't really all that different."

"Quite!"

"Do you ever eat penguins?" Richard asked.

"Now that would be very difficult," Ralop replied, sarcastically.

"Why?"

"Doesn't this boy know anything?" Ralop asked Nilbog in disgust. "It's quite simple. Look around you. Can you see any penguins?"

"Noooo!" Richard admitted.

"Quite - and you won't either. Polar Bears live in the North Pole - where we are now. Penguins live in the South Pole, thousands and thousands of miles away from us. It would mean a very, very long swim if we wanted to find out what penguins tasted like!"

"I suppose it would," Richard replied.

"You know, there's another reason why Polar Bears don't eat penguins," Nilbog added.

"What's that?" asked Richard.

"They can't get the wrappers off!" Nilbog joked. He and Ralop burst out laughing, while Richard looked on, puzzled. Suddenly, he realised what Nilbog meant.

"Oh! Penguin biscuits have wrappers! Of course!" He joined in the laughter.

"What do you call a bear sitting on a mint?" Ralop asked.

"A polo bear!" Richard retorted with another giggle. He knew that one. It was one of his grandfather's favourite jokes, so he'd heard it several times before!

"OK, OK, enough jokes for now, Richard. It's time to go home! Shut your eyes!" Nilbog instructed. Obediently, Richard closed his eyes. The wind whistled around him, and he felt as though he was flying rapidly through the air, then suddenly, he seemed to land firmly on his back. He opened his eyes again, and found himself lying flat on his back in the middle of his bedroom floor.

"W...what happened?" he asked.

"We came home the quick way!" a voice replied. It was Nilbog. "Don't forget to read about your adventure later tonight!"

"What do you mean?"

"In your book. You'll see what I mean when you open it again tonight."

"B ..but ........ I don't like reading. In fact, I *hate* reading . Have I really **got** to read my book **again** tonight?"

"Give it a try. I think you'll be surprised!" Nilbog replied. "Anyway, the magic only works if you read the book! If you don't read it, all the magic will freeze up inside it and I won't be able to come back, so there will be no more adventures. I'll see you again in a day or so, I hope - but you have to keep reading!" There was a flash of sparkly, green light, and Nilbog vanished, as quickly as he had appeared. Richard stared in amazement at the space where his new friend had been standing, then, suddenly he heard his mother's voice floating clearly up the stairs.

"Richard - for the fifth time, will you please turn that television off right now and come down for your tea.  I'm fed up with calling you.  If you don't come downstairs right now I'm giving it to the dog!"

"C...coming Mum," Richard managed to answer. He wandered downstairs, a puzzled expression on his face.

## Chapter 5   Is it in the Book?

That night, Richard's parents were in for another
shock.

Normally, Richard was one of those children who,
like many other boys and girls of his age, never
wanted to go to bed.  He was always ready to
argue for more time - just another five minutes to
finish what he was doing - playing with his Lego
or on his computer; using his Nintendo or
watching something on television.  Bedtime was
one, big argument in his household - normally;
but not tonight!  Tonight everything was different!
For one thing, Richard was a lot quieter than
usual.  Usually he found it hard to sit still for any
length of time, but today he seemed to be
spending a lot of time sitting and thinking -
wondering about what Nilbog had said.  Perhaps
he should try to read his book again tonight.
Maybe there was something special about it, and
maybe the magic did depend on him reading the
book properly.  There was only one way to find
out - whether he liked reading or not, it looked as
though he had no choice.  It wasn't really worth

the risk, anyway.  The promise of four more adventures was very exciting, and he decided that he really would hate to lose them just because he didn't like reading.

Mum looked at Richard, and started to feel concerned.  "It's not like him to be so quiet! Perhaps he's ill - or maybe he's coming down with something." she worried.

"I'm sure he's all right.  He's just plotting some kind of mischief!" Dad replied.

"No, he's never normally as quiet as this.  Do you think I should call a doctor?"

"Has he said that he feels ill?"

"No - but I'm sure something's wrong.  He didn't want a snack after school today!"

"No, but he ate his tea. I saw him!  He nearly had as much as me!" Dad remarked.  "Anyway, he's old enough to tell us if he's ill now so stop fussing!"

"I suppose he is really.  I just worry about him! It's not like him to be so quiet!"  She sat back and continued watching Eastenders.  "It'll be bedtime when this is over, Richard," she added.

"OK Mum," Richard replied, happily. "Can I read my book for a while when I'm in bed?" His parents were astounded! Not only was he not arguing about going to bed, but also he actually **wanted** to read! Surely he HAD to be ill?

"Don't forget to brush your teeth and wash your face before you get into bed, will you?" was all Mum could say before Richard had charged out of the room and up the stairs! His parents just looked at one another.

"What's going on?" Dad asked.

"Perhaps it's that new reading book Mr James found him!" Mum replied. "He's been acting weird since he got it! It seems to be about a boy called Richard who has a magic book. Perhaps he thinks it's real, and this one's going to come alive in his hands too!" she joked.

"You never know," Dad replied, with a smile. "Stranger things have happened!"

"If it makes him want to read, I don't care what it is!" Mum remarked, quietly.

Once upstairs, Richard raced through the bathroom in record time, grabbed his book and jumped into bed, ready to read.

## Chapter 3

Slowly, Richard wandered through to his bedroom - but he didn't switch on the T.V. - not yet.  He had too much to think about.  If HE were writing a magic book with magic adventures, where would he go first?  There were just so many things to choose from - it was too much for his brain to think about. He lay on his bed and closed his eyes to try and think.

Suddenly, he heard someone softly calling his name.  He opened his eyes, and there in front of him was a small, green, elf like creature with large, sticking out ears and a floppy green cap.
"Richard!"
"Who are you?  What are you doing in my room?"
"I'm Nilbog, and I've come to take you on a magical adventure!"
"A m... m... magical adventure?" Richard stammered.  "But where exactly are we going? And how? And for how long?

"This just gets stranger and stranger," thought Richard to himself, as he settled back to read all about his amazing flying adventure and his meeting with Ralop the Polar Bear. "Whatever will happen next?"

## Chapter 6    Can I cheat?

The next morning, Richard woke up early for once.  He was far too excited to sleep any more.  This magic book was such fun!  His first adventure had been amazing, and he couldn't wait for the next one to begin.  Slowly he picked up the book.  Would his last adventure still be in there?  He flicked through the earlier pages.  They all seemed the same.  Soon, he reached Chapter 3 - yesterday's adventure, and slowly he read the chapter through again.  It was all still there - even the jokes (and they still made him giggle!)  Then, as soon as he had finished it, he started to think about what might happen next.  He was beginning to be convinced.  It really was happening!  The book really was magic, and he could hardly wait for the next adventure to happen!

When would it happen, he wondered?  What would it be?  He picked up the book and held it tightly for a few minutes - then suddenly he had an idea!  Perhaps he could cheat a bit and read ahead.  Perhaps he could find out about his next adventure before it even happened!  That would

be exciting!  Nilbog need never know, need he?
He turned over the page - and received another
huge shock as he read what was written.


## Chapter 4

The next morning, Richard woke up
early.  He was too excited to sleep any
more.  This magic book was such fun!
His first adventure had been amazing,
and he couldn't wait for the next one
to begin.  Slowly he picked up the book
and read the last chapter - yesterday's
adventure.  Then, he started to think
about the next one.  When would it
happen? he wondered.  What would it
be?  He picked up the book and held it
tightly for a few minutes - then
suddenly  he had an idea.  Perhaps he
could cheat a bit and read ahead.
Perhaps he could find out what his next
adventure was going to be before it
even happened!  That would be
exciting!  That would be really fun!
Nilbog need never know, need he?

But Nilbog **did** know.  Nilbog knew
everything that was going on, and
there was no way that Richard would
be able to read about an adventure that
had not yet happened.  No-one should

ever be able to read about their own future, even if it was magic!  Richard would just have to wait!

Worriedly, Richard turned the page - but it was empty.  There was nothing there - no writing and no pictures.  The page was totally blank!  He flicked through the next few pages.   There was nothing on any of the pages ahead either.  Richard started to panic.  Had anything been there in the first place, he wondered.  Had his impatience ruined the magic?  He looked back through the earlier pages - fortunately they were all still there; but still he was in a panic.  Nilbog knew that he had tried to cheat.  What if he never came again?  What if he had broken all the magic by trying to cheat?  Why did he do it?  Quickly, Richard stuffed the book back into his backpack.  He was really very worried now.  Perhaps trying to read too much was as bad as not reading at all - it might even be worse!  But as he closed his bag, he heard a quiet, reassuring voice, which seemed to be coming from the book.

"Don't worry, Richard!  I'll see you tonight, but don't try to cheat.  It won't work!"

## Chapter 7   Under the Sea

Wednesday night was bath night for Richard.  He loved bath-times normally, but tonight, unusually for him, he was a little reluctant; after all, he might miss out on an adventure, and that would never do!  Still, his mother had insisted.  "You can jolly well get in that bath and have a good wash. Your book will still be there when you get out, and so will the television; so you won't miss anything," she had said in a very firm tone of voice, and so Richard had to have a bath!  You don't argue with mothers when they say that sort of thing ... not if you know what's good for you!

"I don't want to see you come out of that bathroom for at least 15 minutes," she added. "You had football today, and you're always covered in mud after football.  Make sure you're properly clean - and don't forget to wash your hair!"

 Richard ran the water nice and deep, and jumped in; then he lay back and closed his eyes.  It only took a couple of minutes to wash, so he might as well use the rest of the time thinking about his

adventures and where he would like to go. He
had only been lying there for a minute or so when
there was a loud 'ping' and another sudden flash
of green light. Richard opened his eyes, startled
to find Nilbog standing there in front of him!
"Ready for adventure number 2?" he asked.
"B ... but I'm in the bath!" replied Richard,
shocked.
"Not a problem," Nilbog replied. "We're going
underwater today! Put these on, quickly!" To
Richard's great surprise, Nilbog was holding out a
magical pair of sparkly green swimming trunks.
"Quickly now; we haven't got all day! Good, now
make room for a little one in there with you!"
Nilbog pinched his nose and jumped into the bath
as quick as a flash then, with a click of his fingers,
the magic began! The water changed to a bluey-
green colour and, before Richard's very eyes, the
bottom of the bath vanished and he found himself
under the sea! To his great astonishment, he
found that he could breathe easily - even though
he wasn't wearing all the usual stuff that divers
normally had to wear.

"How come I can breathe underwater, Nilbog?" he asked. "I thought only fish could do that!"

"That's magic for you!" Nilbog replied. "You'll be amazed what magic can do!"

"Where are we going?" Richard continued. He couldn't stop asking questions; but as he asked, he already knew what the answer would be!

"Wait and see!" came the reply, just as he had expected.

They floated through the greeny-blue water, past fishes of all colours, shapes and sizes and through the forests of green, waving seaweed, until suddenly Richard heard a long, deep singing noise - almost like a humming sound. It paused, then started up again.

"What's that sound?" he asked Nilbog.

"It's only a whale," Nilbog replied. "He's singing to tell his friends where he's going. They do it a lot, you know. If you listen carefully, you may hear the reply!"

"Can we go find them? They sound quite close!" Richard asked.

"Not that one. That's a Blue Whale. They are absolutely huge, and they have the loudest voices of any animal in the world. That one could be hundreds of miles away already. We'd never catch up with it!"

"Don't be silly, Nilbog! How could we hear an animal hundreds of miles away? And don't say 'That's magic for you!'"

"I won't - because it isn't. One Blue Whale can hear another's song more than 800 kilometres away. They really do have very loud voices!"

"They must have!" Richard laughed. "My Mum's always complaining that I have a loud voice! I bet she couldn't even hear me at the other end of the street, let alone hundreds of kilometres away! Wait till I tell her about Blue Whales!"

"They have big mouths in more ways than one!" Nilbog added. "Did you know that a Blue Whale's tongue weighs more than a fully grown elephant?"

"You're joking! Good grief! They must be really heavy! How can they carry a tongue that size around with them? I wonder how much they weigh!" Richard paused for a moment before asking, "Nilbog, do you think we will see any whales while we're under here?"

"I'm not sure, Richard. Probably. We'll just have to......"

"Don't say it" Richard butted in. "I know - wait and see!"

"You've got it!" Nilbog replied. "I knew you'd get there in the end!"

"Hey, Nilbog," Richard asked, suddenly thinking of another of his grandfather's jokes. "Do you know where you go to find out how heavy a Blue Whale really is?"

"No," Nilbog replied. "Where do you go?"

"To a whale weigh station!" Richard replied with a giggle. Nilbog laughed too.

"Very good," he said, "but do you know what lies on the bottom of the sea and shivers?"

"No," Richard replied. "What lies at the bottom of the sea and shivers?"

"A nervous wreck!" Nilbog replied. "Let's see if we can find one!" They both giggled as they swam on, further and further, deeper and deeper, chasing the silvery bubbles of their breath and the colourful flashes of the fish around them until suddenly, in front of them, they saw the massive shadow of the enormous wooden wreck of a very old ship.

"Wow!" Richard gasped. "Can we go in there?"

"Where did you think we were going?" Nilbog asked. "I knew you would want to explore this one."

## Chapter 8   Inside The Wreck

Carefully, they edged their way into the huge wreck. Bits of wood were jutting out all around. They twisted and turned, weaving their way through the many areas and playing hide and seek among the rocks. It was such fun to be swimming through this wreck! Suddenly, Richard paused. Something was singing the most beautiful song he had ever heard, but who could it be so far below the water? Slowly, carefully he crept forward. The voice was getting louder, and he knew that he had to be getting closer to its owner. It was unlike anything that Richard had ever heard before! It was amazing! He tried to swim closer, but then he felt Nilbog grab hold of his foot.

Desperately, he tried to shake him off. He just **had** to get to the music. He **had** to listen to it some more.

"Richard!" Nilbog whispered, keeping a firm hold on his foot. "Don't go any closer. You'll frighten them!"

"Why?" Richard asked. "Who are they? What is singing that amazing song?"

"It's the mer-people. They have lived on this wreck for well over a hundred years - they feel safe here. It's so far down that very few earth people ever come this far, and those that do rarely hear them."

"Mer-people? But they aren't real, are they? I thought they were just made up things - from stories!"

"Nope. They're as real as I am! It's only people who have never seen them or heard them who say that they don't exist - just like those people who say that elves and goblins don't exist! Some people only believe in things that they can see with their own eyes."

"Can we go any closer?"

"Only if you're very, very quiet. If they hear the slightest sound, they will hide! They're very nervous creatures."

Slowly, almost silently, Richard and Nilbog edged forwards. In front of them, a huge, wooden door stood ajar. They crept towards it, barely breathing; trying hard to be as silent as possible, and peered round the door into a vast ballroom, decorated with shells, seaweed, and many beautiful treasures that the mer-people had discovered over the years. In front of them, at the other end of the ballroom was a huge throne and, seated on it, was a large, powerful looking mer-man. He was holding a three pronged, golden trident.

"That's Triton. He's the King of the mer-people," Nilbog whispered, almost silently. Many other mer-men and mer-women were dancing and singing in front of Triton's throne. Richard just sat there, watching and listening, barely able to move from the spot. "Over the years, many sailors have felt like you do about their music," Nilbog added. "It is beautiful, but you mustn't listen to it for too long, or you will never want to leave, and that would never do!"

All of a sudden, the mermaids stopped singing and began to dart around the ballroom anxiously. "What's happened? Why have they stopped? Have we frightened them?" Richard asked, concerned. "Not us, look!" Nilbog whispered back. An enormous, grey shadow fell across the ballroom.

## Chapter 9  Krash!

Richard looked up.  Just ahead of him, a huge, grey shark with the most enormous, sharp, pointed teeth was squeezing into the wreck! Terrified mer-people were swimming all over, searching for hiding places, calling to one another to take care.  King Triton dived behind his throne, dropping his trident on the floor in his panic. Other mer-people hid where ever they could find shelter - under tables and behind rocks. Anywhere that was too small for the shark to follow became a hiding space for a frightened mer-man or woman, mermaid or mer-boy.

"Quickly, come over here!" Nilbog called to Richard.  "We must hide!  It's too dangerous to stay out here."  They dived for cover behind a nearby rock.  As Richard peered out, he could see the last few mer-people still swimming about quickly, hunting for a safe place to hide.  One of them, a small mer-boy about the same age as Richard, dived behind the rock where Richard and Nilbog were hiding.  He looked at them in horror, and would have dived straight back out again into the terrifyingly sharp jaws of the shark if Richard hadn't grabbed him by the arm and held on to him tightly.  The mer-boy struggled, but he couldn't escape. Richard continued to hold on firmly, but the mer-boy started to panic, and opened his mouth to shout for help.

 "Shh!  It's all right," Richard said quickly, trying to reassure him.  "We're friends.  We don't want to hurt you, but you must stay here until the shark has gone!  He looks fierce - and hungry!" "He always is," the boy replied as he stopped struggling, but still Richard kept hold of his arm - he didn't want him to escape and run into the jaws of the shark!  "He keeps coming here in search for food, and we have to keep hiding from him!"  The boy paused again.  He didn't look quite as worried now.  "Who are you, and where have you come from?  What are you doing here?" he demanded, so Richard told him his name, and told him a little about the magic book and his adventures.  "Wow!  That sounds like fun!" the boy remarked.  "I wish I had a magic book.  I'd ask it to take me to the land of the earth people, so I could see what life is like there.  I've always wanted to know more about how the humans live!"

"What is your name?" Richard asked.

"Aquarius," the boy replied.  "All our names have something to do with water.  My name means 'water carrier'.  What does your name mean?"

"I'm not sure," Richard replied.  "I've never really thought about it before.  I'll have to try and find out!"  He peered out from behind the rock again, and jumped back quickly.  "He's still there!  What do you normally do when he's around?"

"We stay hidden until he gives up," Aquarius replied.  "It takes a while, but eventually he'll decide to go somewhere else for dinner."

"Have you tried any other way to get rid of him?" Richard asked.

"Like what?"

"I'm not sure, but if we worked together, I'm sure we could find a way!" Richard replied.  "Let's think!" They sat for a while, thinking hard, until all at once Richard said: "Got it!" He whispered his plan to Aquarius and Nilbog. "What do you think? Could we do it?" he asked.

"We'd have to be very, very careful," Nilbog replied. "If either of us got eaten by a shark, this book would have to come to a very sudden end, and a lot of people, including your parents, Richard, would be extremely disappointed!"

"Of course we will! None of us want to end up as shark food, thank you very much!" Richard retorted. "Anyway - remember what you said, Nilbog. Anything can happen in magic adventures if we believe it, and I **know** we can do it!"

"I'm sure some of the others would help when they realised what we were doing, anyway!" Aquarius added.

"OK," Richard said. "Are we ready?"


Bravely, Richard and Aquarius swam out together from behind the rock where they were hiding. Quietly, Richard swam over to the throne and picked up the trident that King Triton had dropped in his rush to hide. Silently, he crept up behind the large fish, then suddenly he attacked and jabbed him firmly in the tail with the sharp points of the trident. As the shark tried to turn his huge body to see what was stinging him, Richard quickly threw the trident to Aquarius, who swam to the other side of the shark's body, and jabbed again - this time in his enormous tummy. Quickly and carefully, he threw the trident back to Richard. It wouldn't do to drop it at this stage! Richard grabbed it and jabbed the shark's tail once again, then the two boys turned and swam off in different directions, as fast as they could. The shark was puzzled for a moment, not knowing which of the two boys to chase, but then he spotted the trident in Richard's hand, and realised what it was that had hurt him so much. Quick as a flash, his tail thrashing the water behind, he turned and began to follow the boy, who darted rapidly back to where Nilbog was waiting behind the rock, whilst Aquarius dashed over to hide behind the throne with a trembling King Triton!

Richard crept backwards into the space, watching the shark nervously and hoping that his plan would work; then, like a flash, he realised that Nilbog's magic was working so well that they could even hear the shark's thoughts!

"Cheeky brat," he was thinking. "I'll show him! I'll have him! It's dinner time, and he's the main course or my name's not Krash the Shark!"

Richard moved further forwards. The gap between the rocks and the side of the ship was quite small, but there was still plenty of room for him to move. Still, he knew that the shark was a lot bigger than him, so the plan should work! Making sure that Krash was still following him, he slipped out through the gap at the other end. The shark continued to follow - until suddenly he found he could swim no more! He was stuck - trapped between the ship and the rock! He started to struggle, wriggling and jiggling his body, but the space seemed to be getting smaller and smaller. Quick as a flash, Nilbog appeared in front of the struggling shark. He clicked his fingers and, before anyone had time to think, the shark suddenly found himself back in the middle of the ballroom in front of King Triton's throne; but this time he was trapped in a strong, metal cage. He struggled and twisted around in the small space, bashing his body against the bars of the cage, frantically trying to escape.

Nilbog let him struggle for a few seconds; then he shouted firmly, "Stop!"
The shark turned to look at him, and Nilbog continued. "Stop struggling, and listen to me, Krash. You are now caught in a magic trap, and there is only one way to escape from it." He paused and looked firmly at the shark. "You have a choice. Either you promise here and now that you will leave these mer-people alone and not bother them again, in which case I will let you go free, or you don't promise and have to stay in this cage forever!" Still, the shark wriggled, and bashed his body firmly against the metal bars over and over again. There had to be another way out, he thought. There had to be a way to escape! But

the more he struggled, the smaller and tighter the cage seemed to become.

"Think about it, Krash: the rest of your life in a cage being fed the occasional fish; or freedom. Which would you prefer?" The shark wriggled once more, but he was beginning to realise that there was no way that he could escape from Nilbog's magic cage. All around, nervous mer-people were creeping carefully, bit by bit, out of their hiding places to watch the trapped shark. He eyed them all hungrily, and they drew back again, still a little frightened of its sharp teeth. "Perhaps I could just pretend to agree," Krash thought, not realising that everyone could hear him think. "They'd never know!"

But Nilbog surprised him by replying:- "No, Krash. Pretending won't work. If you ever set fin into this wreck again, you'll find yourself trapped in this cage, and I won't be here with the magic words to release you! You have 10 seconds to make your mind up. What are you going to choose?"

The shark paused, and Nilbog started counting.

"Ten, ............, Nine, ............, Eight, .........,
Seven,"

"OK, OK, I promise!" he shouted, quickly.

"You'll never enter this wreck again?" Nilbog
asked.

"I'll never enter this wreck again," Krash promised.

"And you'll never try to eat one of the mer-people
again as long as you live?"

"WHAT!  NEVER?  Not even when they're out of the
ship?"

"Not even then!"  There was another pause.  "I'm
still counting," Nilbog warned the shark.  "Six,
.............. , Five ............, Four, ....."

"All right!  I promise!  Just let me out of this cage,
PLEASE!"

"And you'll never try to chase Richard and me."

"Never," Krash promised again.  He was really
panicking now.  He didn't like the thought of
being a prisoner in this tiny cage for the rest of
his life, and would do anything to get out of it.  "I
promise!  If you'll just let me go!  Sharks aren't
meant to be kept in cages, and I don't like it."

"Remember," Nilbog warned. "A promise is a promise, and promises have to be kept! Break your promise just once, and you'll be back in this cage before you have time to say your name! And next time there will be no easy way out!"

"I'll remember!" the shark promised. "Please, just let me out!"

"Not until you say sorry to King Triton and the rest of the Mer-people for frightening them so much!" There was another brief pause, just long enough for Nilbog to add one word. "Three, ..."

"I'm sorry, I'm sorry!" the shark said quickly. "Please, let me go! I want to go home! I WANT MY MUMMY! I WANT MY BIG SISTER!" And he began to cry. Large shark tears rolled round his cheeks. The mer-people crept closer. Never before had they seen a shark cry! He must have been really scared, they thought.

"Let him out, Nilbog," said King Triton. "I think he's learnt his lesson this time!" Nilbog snapped his fingers, and the cage disappeared as suddenly as it had appeared. Before anyone had time to think, the sobbing shark had turned and fled from the ship, calling loudly for his Mummy as he went.

"Three cheers for Nilbog and Richard!" shouted a small voice.  It was Aquarius!  "They saved us from the shark!"

"And three cheers for my grandson, Aquarius," King Triton added.  "I saw what you did to help, my boy, and I'm proud of you!"   Richard looked at his new friend in astonishment.

"You never said that King Triton was your granddad!" he said.

"You never asked!" Aquarius replied.  The two boys giggled together and gave each other a high five.

"I've got a mer-joke for you, Richard," Aquarius said.  "Do you know what sea monsters eat?"

"No, what do they eat?" Richard asked.  He was enjoying all these jokes. He couldn't wait to try them out on his grandfather, and on his friends at school as well!

"Fish and ships!" came the reply.  Richard laughed again.

"Time to go, Richard," Nilbog announced. "Your bath will be getting cold!"

"What's a bath?" Aquarius asked, intrigued. He had never heard of one of those before, and was keen to know more about human life.

"Something that you will never need," Richard replied. "It's a big tub. We fill it with water and then we wash ourselves in it! I'm going to have to go - but it's really been fun!"

"It certainly has," Aquarius replied. "Will you come back and see us some time?"

"I don't know," Richard answered, "but I hope so! You'll have to ask Nilbog!"

"Wait and see," Nilbog replied. "You never know!" He clicked his fingers once more, and before Richard had time to blink, the wreck and all the mer-people had vanished, and he was back in his bath with Nilbog standing by the side.

"Don't forget to read about your adventure tonight!" Nilbog said.

"I won't! I know I have to. Even if I do hate books normally, this one's different! I've found that out already!" There was a sudden flash of green light, and Nilbog vanished.  Richard lay back in his bath and closed his eyes, but before he had time to think, he heard his mother's voice outside the door.

"Richard, are you all right in there?" she asked. "You've been there for nearly half an hour!  Surely you must be clean by now!"

"Sorry, Mum," he said, jumping quickly out of the bath. "I must have fallen asleep or something! Just coming!"

"This is really weird," he thought as he dried himself off and took off his magic swimming trunks, "but it's rather fun!  I hope it keeps going!"

## Chapter 10   I Know I shouldn't, but ...

By the time Richard got out of the bath and into his pyjamas, it was already bedtime.   He could hear his mother on her way upstairs to say 'Good night', and bring him up a glass of chocolate milk, so hurriedly he stuffed the magic swimming trunks under his pillow before she could come in and start asking awkward questions.  Amazingly enough, they were already dry!

"Can I read for a little while?" Richard asked.

"No, Richard," his mother told him.  "It's late already, and you have school in the morning."

"Oh please, Mum.  Just for a little while!  I'm not sleepy yet - really I'm not!"

"Perhaps five minutes or so then if you promise to turn your light out as soon as we tell you," his mother agreed. "But not for long, or you'll never want to get up tomorrow.  You know what you're like in the mornings!"

Mornings were never a good time for Richard.  He hated getting up even more than he hated going to bed at night, and Mum always had problems persuading him to get out of bed!  She often had to resort to pulling the bedclothes off, and once she had even threatened to throw cold water over him if he didn't hurry up and get up, but it was so nice to see him actually **wanting** to read that she didn't really want to put him off.

Richard picked up his book and snuggled down under the bedclothes to read, hoping that his new adventure would be in there already. He turned the pages carefully, until he found the right place.

## Chapter 5

Wednesday night was bath night for Richard but, unusually for him, tonight he was a little reluctant. After all, he might miss out on an adventure, and that would never do! Still, his mother insisted. "You can jolly well get in that bath and have a good wash. Your book will still be there when you get out, and so will the television, so you won't miss anything," she said firmly, and so Richard had to have a bath! "I don't want to see you come out of that bathroom for at least 15 minutes," she added. "You had football today, and you're always covered in mud after football. Make sure you're properly clean - and don't forget to wash your hair!"

Richard ran the water nice and deep, and jumped in, then he laid back and closed his eyes.  It only took a couple of minutes to wash, so he might as well use the rest of the time thinking about his adventures and where he would like to go. He had only been laying there for a minute or so when there was a sudden flash of green light.  Richard opened his eyes, startled to find Nilbog standing there in front of him.

Richard read on, excitedly.  He had just reached the part where the mer-people had stopped singing and had started to swim about desperately to find somewhere to hide, when he heard his mother shout up "OK Richard!  Lights out now!  It's time to stop reading and go to sleep, please!"

"Oh no!" Richard thought.  "It's not fair!  Just as I got to the exciting bit!  I can't stop now.  Just five minutes more.  I've got to just get to the end of this bit!"

Eagerly, naughtily, he turned the page - but Nilbog had got their first! He must have known what would happen, and so the next page was still blank. The next chapter was not in the book yet! He heard a click, as if someone had clicked their fingers, and his bedroom light flashed off. "You meanie, Nilbog!" he muttered. "I might have guessed! I was at the exciting bit too!"

"You know what I said, Richard," came Nilbog's voice from out of the darkness. "No cheating! You promised your mother! Like we told Krash, a promise is a promise, and promises have to be kept. Nothing more will be written in that book until morning. You will be able to finish reading about today's adventure when you wake up tomorrow - and not before."

"OK Nilbog. I'm sorry. I shouldn't have tried to cheat." Richard put the book down onto the floor by the side of his bed and settled down to go to sleep.

"Goodnight, Richard!" Nilbog said.

"Goodnight Nilbog; and thank you!" Richard replied. He closed his eyes, and within seconds

he was asleep and dreaming of undersea worlds
with singing whales, mer-people and sharks.

## Chapter 11 It's there!

The next morning, Richard woke up bright and early for once. At first, he couldn't think why he was feeling so excited, then suddenly he remembered - the book! The next chapter should have been written by now! After all, Nilbog **did** promise - and, as he was learning, a promise is a promise! Eagerly, he reached down beside the bed and grabbed his book. Quickly, he flicked through the pages until he came to the start of chapter 6, and started to read about his fantastic adventure.

To his huge surprise, it was almost as exciting to read about his adventure as it had been in real life! He hadn't forgotten how frightening the shark had been, with its huge, pointed teeth, or how terrified the mer-people had seemed. He hadn't forgotten his own fear as he had looked into the steely, grey eyes and long, pointed nose of the shark, or as he'd been swimming for his life with the shark following close behind. Still, it was amazing to think that the story he was reading was all about his own adventures. No-one would ever believe him - after all, he could hardly believe it himself! It was all just too incredible to be true!

"That was some adventure!" he said to himself. "I wonder what will happen next?"

"Wait and see," came Nilbog's voice - seemingly from nowhere. "It won't be long!"

## Chapter 12   The Magic Continues

All that day at school, Richard was restless and fidgety - even more so than usual.  He couldn't wait to get home; after all, Nilbog **had** promised that it wouldn't be long to his next adventure, and the last one had been so super!  He kept remembering little things, and once or twice, had found it hard to stop himself from laughing!  Mr James had to keep reminding him to get on with his work and to concentrate (OK, so perhaps that wasn't so unusual really!  He didn't have the best concentration skills in the class!)  Still, the end of the day just couldn't come soon enough for Richard today.  He was desperate to find out what Nilbog had planned for him today, and couldn't wait to get home to find out.  The day just seemed to drag on.  Minutes seemed like hours, and the bells seemed to be ringing later and later.  Richard was feeling increasingly restless, until it came to their art lesson!

It was the last hour or so of the day, and Mr James handed everyone a piece of paper and said to them all, "I want you to imagine that you are swimming under the sea.  Draw what you can see there.  I've put some books around the room to help you."  Richard looked up, amazed.  Could Mr James possibly know about his adventure last night?  Surely not!  He looked around the room.  There were all sorts of books scattered around with pictures of fish and dolphins, sharks and whales; but he didn't need any of them.  He already knew exactly what he was going to draw.  He was going to draw the shipwreck, with Aquarius and Triton and all the other mer-people - and, of course, the shark - before they had captured it!  He reached for the packet of felt tip pens and began.  He was so wrapped up in his picture that, for once that day, time seemed to fly past, and he felt almost sad when Mr James told them to tidy up quickly because it was nearly home time.  The teacher looked carefully at Richard's picture as he collected it in.  "This is lovely.  You really do have a vivid imagination when you want to use it, Richard!" he commented.

When the bell finally rang, Richard threw his books into his drawer and charged out of the room to the school gates, where his Mum was waiting.

"Hello, Richard.  You're ready quickly!  Did you have a nice day?" she asked, taking his lunchbox and backpack from him.

"OK, I suppose," Richard replied.  "Can we go?"

Richard and his mother set off for home.

All of a sudden, it started to rain - not just fine drizzle, but really heavy rain - the sort that soaks you all the way through.  Richard and his mother hurried home and into the kitchen.  "Straight upstairs and out of those wet clothes, Richard!" his mother told him, "then I'll make us a nice, hot cup of tea to warm us up!"

Richard charged upstairs into the bathroom to throw the wet clothes into the linen basket and dry himself off, then straight back to his bedroom to throw on clean jeans and a 't' shirt, much more comfortable than his school uniform any day!  Suddenly he heard a funny little noise.  He turned round and there, perched on the bottom of his bed, was Nilbog!

"What are you doing here?" Richard demanded in surprise. "How long have you been sitting there?"

"Just a little while," Nilbog replied. "I wondered how long it would take you to notice me!"

"What if my mother had come in?"

"She wouldn't have seen me. Grown-ups are quite blind when it comes to seeing magical creatures. They never believe in anything they haven't already seen for themselves and, as you can only ever see things that you already believe in, it's very rare that a grown-up will ever see us!"

"That's lucky!" Richard replied. "Does that mean that she'll never see the magical swimming trunks either?" He giggled. "What'll happen if I wear them for swimming on Saturday?"

"No chance of that," Nilbog retorted. "They've gone back to where they came from already! You don't need them anymore!"

"OH! I was looking forwards to showing them to my friends!"

"Sorry, Richard. Not allowed. You can't bring any magical souvenirs back with you. You never know what they might get up to!"

"I suppose so!" Richard agreed. "Hey - is it time for our next adventure yet?"

"Certainly is!" Nilbog replied.

"Where are we going?"

"Wait and see!" Nilbog replied. "Grab my coat, and off we go!"

Richard reached out to grab hold of Nilbog's coat tails. As he touched them, the room seemed to spin round, then everything was spinning - it was like being caught up in a whirlwind! Richard held on firmly as everything swirled round - then, just as suddenly, he found himself flat on his back in the middle of a clearing in the most unusual forest that he had ever seen!

## Chapter 13   Fantasy Land

Richard rubbed his eyes, unsure whether he could really believe what he saw.  This forest was amazing!  It was full of glittery, silver coloured trees covered with pink, purple and pale blue leaves - and, instead of fruits growing on the trees, there were ... all kinds of different coloured sweets!  Richard looked on, amazed.

"Do you want to help yourself to a couple, Richard?" Nilbog asked.

"Can I?"

"Of course!  This is Fantasy Land.  Try what you want - but remember, you can't take any of it home.  It all belongs here!  That's part of the magic!"

Richard reached out to pick an orange coloured sweet from one of the trees.  He put it in his mouth.  It was delicious!  Very different from any other orange sweet that he had ever tasted before.  It was sort of fizzy and creamy at the same time - a bit like fresh orange and lemonade - but with something else added - a mysterious, mystical flavour and, although it was hard on the outside, when he bit into it the centre was deliciously soft and chewy.  He picked a green one.  It tasted like a sparkly lemon and lime soda, fizzing up and finally bursting on his tongue in a wonderful explosion of flavours.

"Try one of the twigs!" Nilbog suggested.  Richard did so.

"Wow!" he gasped.  It was the creamiest, silkiest milk chocolate that he had ever tasted!  He took another.  "We'd better not stay here too long, Nilbog!" he remarked.  "I'll be as fat as a pig!  This is the most delicious place I have ever visited!"

"There's lots more to see!" Nilbog replied.  Richard reached out to pick a few more of the sweets - just so that he could say that he'd tasted one of every flavour.  It would be awful to go home wondering what - say - the purple ones taste like.

"Can we eat the leaves as well?" he asked.

"Try them and see," Nilbog replied - so Richard did!  They were just like huge lollipops!  He licked away at one - a blue one.  It tasted of bubble gum.  He bit a bit off and chewed it - it was chewy like bubble gum, so he tried blowing a bubble.  It grew larger and larger and larger - the largest he had ever blown. He felt his feet slowly lifting up off the ground. He was flying! He stopped blowing for a second, and felt himself drop until his feet were touching the ground again. Quickly, he burst the bubble.

"Nilbog, did you see that?" he asked.

"What?" Nilbog asked.

"This!" Richard blew again. As the bubble grew, his feet started to lift off from the ground until... once again he was hovering about a metre above the floor! He twisted and turned, flying upside down and looping the loop, until his bubble started to lose air again and he floated gently back down to the ground.

"I see you've discovered the bubble gum tree!" Nilbog remarked, as Richard dropped back down to earth again. "It's fun, isn't it? The last boy I brought here - must be about 20 years ago now - he had fun with the bubble tree as well!"

"You mean other children have had adventures like these as well?"

"Not exactly the same as yours - but yes, they've had adventures. Where we go and what we do is special to you - but Fantasy Land is a favourite of mine. I try to bring all my special friends here."

"Will everyone who reads this book have these adventures?" Richard asked

"No. This is your book. It's being written especially for you. These are your adventures - no-one else's."

"How do you choose who has the adventures?"

"The books choose. This one chose you!" Nilbog replied.

"But ... what if Mr James had given it to someone else?"

"He couldn't have. It had your name on it didn't it?"

"I suppose it did! I was really lucky there!"

"Yes, you were. Come on now. There's a lot more to see here. You've hardly seen anything yet!"

Nilbog and Richard set off to wander further into the wonderfully mysterious forest, past amazing tree after amazing tree. Soon Richard began to realise that he would never be able to taste a sweet from every tree, even if he were to be there all year! He tried a few more, but realised that he was beginning to feel very thirsty. He was just about to say something to Nilbog, when he noticed a beautiful waterfall just over to the left of the path. The water was all the colours of the rainbow, and he could hear it tumbling and splashing into the pool at the bottom. It sounded most inviting!

They moved closer to have a better look and, as they walked over, Richard noticed an amazing, golden goblet perched on a stone by the edge of the pond. Nilbog picked it up and dipped it into the water; then he handed it to Richard, who took a sip. It was the most delicious drink that he had ever tasted! All the flavours that he loved were combined in this amazing concoction! Strawberries, raspberries, cola, all sorts of things. He had another sip. It was just as delicious, but now he could taste even more wonderful flavours! Richard could hardly believe it.

"It's magical!" he gasped, looking at Nilbog. "It's the most magical thing I have ever drunk!"

"It is pretty amazing," Nilbog agreed. "We call it Rainbow Juice, and these falls are the Fantasy Rainbow Falls." Richard drank the rest of the Rainbow Juice in the goblet, then, almost greedily, he refilled it and drank some more. If only all drinks could taste like this!

Suddenly, they heard a funny noise. It was like a cross between a whinny and a neigh. Richard looked around to see what was making the noise, but he could see nothing.

"What is it, Nilbog?" Richard asked, putting the goblet back down on the rock. "What's making that noise?"

Nilbog's reply amazed him!

# Chapter 14  Nicornu

"Have you got any of the pink sweets in your pockets?"

"Yes. Why?"

"Eat one now, then you'll understand what's going on. It's Nicornu, and he's upset for some reason. Only a child can help him, - but unless you eat one of the pink sweets first, he'll be frightened of you and he'll run away."

"Who's Nicornu?"

"You'll see in a minute. Hurry up and eat one of those pink sweets!" Richard searched through the mass of sweets in his pocket, and pulled out one of the pink ones. Shoving it into his mouth, he started to chew and, as the delicious raspberry flavour exploded onto his tongue, he suddenly realised that Nicornu, whoever he was, was crying! Nilbog and Richard walked further forwards, and found themselves in another clearing. Richard gasped with amazement, for there, in front of him, was ... a Unicorn!  It was the most beautiful animal that Richard had ever seen. His legs were long and slender, leading up to a silky, silvery white, glistening body.  His mane and tail were so golden, they seemed to glisten and sparkle in the sunlight and, sticking out from the centre of his forehead, was a single, golden coloured horn. Carefully, gently, Richard went up to the beautiful creature.  As he got closer, he could see the rainbow coloured tears rolling down its face.  He couldn't help himself.  He reached out and touched Nicornu's silky mane with his finger tips. "What's wrong," he whispered.  "Why are you crying?"

The Unicorn jumped back, startled.

"Who are you?" it demanded.  "What are you doing here?"

"Nilbog brought me," Richard replied.  "See, he's over there.  We were worried about you.  What's the matter?"  Somehow, Richard knew that seeing Nilbog would help this shy, nervous creature. "Can we help?"

"No-one can help.  It's the annual Unicorn race today, and my rider hasn't turned up, so I can't take part.  And it's the first year that I've been old enough to enter." Nicornu sobbed. "Oh, it's just not fair!"

"Can't you take part without a rider?" Richard asked.

"No. That's one of the rules. Every Unicorn must have a rider. Without a rider, I can't enter. Nilbog is too old, so I can't use him."

"How about you, Richard?" Nilbog asked. "Could you do it?"

"Me?" Richard replied with a gasp of amazement. "But I've never ridden a Unicorn before. I've never even ridden a horse! I wouldn't know what to do!"

"Nicornu knows what to do; but riding a Unicorn is nothing like riding a horse. Unicorns are proud, masterful creatures. They don't let just anyone ride them, and so when you ride a Unicorn, it's the Unicorn who's in charge, not the rider. Anyway I've told you before, in magical adventures, you can do anything! Just sit on his back and let him do all the work."

Richard turned to Nicornu. "What do you think, Nicornu? Could we do it? Would you let me be your rider?"

"W ... w... would you like to?" Nicornu asked, hopefully.

"Of course I would," Richard replied with a smile, "if you don't mind taking me, that is."

"D ... d ... do you want to try first? You m ... m ... might not like it," Nicornu worried.

"I'm sure I will," Richard replied "but you're right - it would be best for both of us if I had a ride now, before the race. How do I get on?"

"Like this!" Nilbog replied, and he clicked his fingers. Before Richard had time to think what he was doing, he found himself perched on Nicornu's back.

"What do I hold?" he asked.

"Hold my mane!" Nicornu replied. "Off we go!" They started with a gentle trot, bouncing around the clearing. It was so gentle; it was like riding a toy Unicorn on a merry-go-round. Gradually, Nicornu got faster and faster, until he was galloping. Richard felt almost as if he were flying! The wind whistled around his face and he grew more and more excited, as he realised that he could hardly feel Nicornu's feet touch the ground.

"This is amazing!" he shouted. "Can we go any faster, Nicornu?"

"Of course I can!" Nicornu replied, feeling more confident now. "Wait till the race; then you'll see how fast a unicorn can go!" They slowed down and stopped, just in front of Nilbog.

"Have you seen the time?" Nilbog asked. "We'd better be going! The race starts in half an hour!" He looked at Nicornu. "Do you want to take Richard, and I'll come on by myself?" he asked. The Unicorn gave a whinny of delight.

"I'd love that, if you don't mind!" he replied.

"Yes please," replied Richard, and they set off, galloping through the forest. The wonderfully coloured trees seemed to flash past as Nicornu raced on. Soon they reached another, much larger clearing, where Richard was amazed to see what looked like hundreds of Unicorns, all with a rider on their backs, and in the centre of the group stood a small elf, who was standing on a large tree trunk. Nicornu raced up to the elf.

"Am I too late?" he demanded, almost breathlessly. "Please don't say I'm too late! I've got a rider now." The elf looked at his wrist - Richard was amazed to see that he was wearing a watch!

"Just in time!" he declared. "Your race begins in 15 minutes. Go and get ready!" Nicornu gave a little whinny of delight, and trotted over to join a group of Unicorns all with the same colouring as his own.

"Hiya Nicornu!" said one of the unicorns. "I'm glad you made it. We wondered where you'd got to, and I was beginning to think that you were going to miss the race!"

"So did I, Norcu," Nicornu replied. "I nearly didn't have a rider!"

"That would have been dreadful," Norcu replied. "It would be awful to miss your first ever Unicorn race!"

"It certainly would," Nicornu replied.

Richard looked around the clearing. All the Unicorns were in groups, and all the groups were slightly different. One group had silvery coloured manes, another had silvery manes and tails, and a third group also had silver horns.

"Why do the Unicorns in that group have different coloured horns and manes from you and your friends, Nicornu?" asked Richard.

"They're a lot older," Nicornu replied. "As we grow older, our colourings change. When I was born, my whole body was golden, instead of being silvery white. It changed gradually over the last three years until it was this colour. Over the next year, my mane will go silvery, then my tail the year after. The last thing that changes is my horn, and when that happens, I will be a fully grown Unicorn."

"Where does everyone get their riders from?"

"We use some of the fairies, gnomes and elves who live in the forests, but my elf was ill today," said Nicornu. "I'm glad you came, Richard!"

"So'm I," replied Richard with a smile. Suddenly, Nilbog appeared among them.

"So, are you ready?" he asked.

"I th...think so," Nicornu replied, nervously.

"I'm sure so," said Richard, confidently. "Look at the speed that we came through the forest! We nearly flew!"

"That's true."

"Anyway, it'll be fun.  Mum always says 'It's not the winning that matters.  Taking part is far more important!'"

"I suppose so," Nicornu agreed. "But it would be nice to win!"

"They're calling your group to the starting line, Nicornu!" remarked Nilbog.  "Off you go.  Good luck, and have fun both of you!"

"We will!" Richard replied as Nicornu trotted over for the start of the race.  When they were all lined up, the starter elf pulled a whistle out of his pocket and held it, ready.

"Is everybody here?" he asked.  Everyone nodded. "Right.  The race starts when I blow my whistle. The course is marked out by shiny, silver stars on the path. Follow the magic course through the forest and back to here.  Good luck, everybody! May the fastest Unicorn win!"  The Unicorns all gave a gentle whinny.

"Are you ready, Richard?" Nicornu asked.

"Ready and waiting!" Richard replied.  The elf put the whistle to his lips, and the Unicorns all began

to paw the ground. "Three, ....Two, .... One, ...,"
he counted, and then he blew the whistle. They
were off!

If Richard had found his earlier rides amazing, this
was even better! Nicornu's feet barely seemed to
touch the ground as they nearly flew round the
course. Magical, silvery stars flashed past
underneath them as they wove their way around
the trees, twisting and turning as they went.
Richard found himself growing more and more
excited, cheering Nicornu on as they passed
Unicorn after Unicorn. Suddenly they both
realised that there was only one more Unicorn
ahead of them, and it was Norcu!

"Come on, Nicornu!" Richard shouted. "You can
do it! Keep going!" The little Unicorn kept
ploughing on, further and further forwards. There
were only centimetres between him and Norcu
now; but the winning post was already in sight.
"You're nearly there!" Richard shouted. "You can
do it! Come on!"

Nicornu kicked a little harder, and found himself
going even faster. Richard could feel Nicornu's

heart beating as he ran, but the distance between the two unicorns was getting smaller and smaller. Suddenly they found that they were running next to one another; and then, just before they reached the winning post, Nicornu started to pull ahead! He was in the lead!  Just a few metres to go and Nicornu would win his first ever unicorn race! "Don't give up now, Nicornu!" Richard encouraged him.  "Go, go, go!"  Nicornu pushed himself harder, and suddenly found himself across the finishing line, barely two metres ahead of his friend!

"Hooray!  We've done it!" they both shouted together.  Nilbog and a couple of the other elves came over to congratulate them.  A beautiful fairy in a sparkly golden coloured dress came over and flung a golden medal round Richard's neck, and another stuck a golden rosette to Nicornu's horn. All around them, Unicorns, elves and fairies were celebrating their win.

Norcu and his rider came up.  He was wearing a silver rosette, and his rider had a medal similar to Richard's on his front, but in silver.  "Well done,

Nicornu. Well done Richard." they said. "We thought we'd done it. We couldn't believe it when you came past us like that! Where did you get that final burst of strength from?"

"I don't know!" Nicornu replied. "I just kept going. All the time, I could hear Richard encouraging me on, and somehow I just knew I could do it!"

"You two must have been practising for ages!"

"No, we only met today for the first time!" Nicornu replied. "My elf was ill, and Richard offered to help me out!"

"That's amazing! Watch out, though. We'll beat you next year! We're starting practising tomorrow!"

Suddenly Richard heard Nilbog's voice. "Richard. Time to go home! If we don't go home quickly, your Mum will be wondering where you are!"

"OH!" Richard sighed, loudly. "Do we have to?"

"Yes, Richard," Nilbog replied. "I'm afraid so. Say goodbye to Nicornu and the others. It really is time to go now, I'm afraid."

"OK," Richard sighed, and turned to Nicornu. "Sorry, Nicornu. I have to go home now, but thank you ever so much! It's been brilliant!"

"Richard," Nicornu replied. "It's me who should be thanking you! I couldn't have done any of this without you and Nilbog! If you two hadn't turned up, I'd still be crying! I'll never forget you - or today!"

"Nor will I," Richard replied. "It's been ... magical! Take care, Nicornu!"

"You too, Richard. I hope I'll see you again sometime!"

"You never know, Nicornu. You'll have to ask Nilbog!" Richard replied. He bent down to kiss the sparkling, golden mane; then Nilbog clicked his fingers once more. Once again, everything seemed to spin round until suddenly, Richard found himself sitting on the bottom of his bed next to Nilbog. He looked down and realised that he was still wearing the medal; but it had shrunk! It was tiny - about the same size as a 5p piece!

"You can keep that one, Richard," said Nilbog. "You earned it - just don't show it to your Mum, or she'll wonder what you've been doing!"

"Thanks, Nilbog! That was an amazing adventure!" Richard gasped. He took the medal off and wrapped it round the teddy bear that was sitting on his cupboard. Although he felt he was too old to have a teddy bear in his bed now, he still liked to see it around in his bedroom, and his bear seemed to be the perfect place to 'hide' his medal!

"Don't forget to read about it, will you?" Nilbog reminded him.

"I won't, I promise!" Richard replied. "And a promise is a promise, you know!"

"I see you're learning," said Nilbog, winking a sparkly, green eye. "Well done!" He clicked his fingers again, and disappeared, and Richard wandered downstairs to see if he still had a cup of tea waiting for him.

## Chapter 15   Back to the Book

That night, Richard's parents weren't quite so
surprised when he asked if he could read in bed.
They were beginning to get used to it now,
although they still found it a bit weird.
Once again, Richard charged upstairs and got
himself ready for bed in record time.  Once again,
he grabbed his book and began to read about his
adventures.

### Chapter 7

Richard rubbed his eyes, unsure
whether he could believe what he saw.
This forest was quite amazing.  It was
full of glittery, silver coloured trees
covered with pink, purple and pale blue
leaves - and growing on the trees,
instead of fruits, were ...... all kinds of
different coloured sweets!  Richard
looked on, amazed.

"Do you want to help yourself to a
couple, Richard?" Nilbog asked.

"Can I?" Richard asked.
"Of course!  This is Fantasy Land.  Try
what you want - but remember, you
can't take any of it home.  It all

belongs here!  That's part of the magic!"

Richard reached out to pick an orange coloured sweet from one of the trees. He put it in his mouth.  It was delicious!  Very different from any other orange sweet that he had ever tasted before.  It was sort of fizzy and creamy at the same time - a bit like fresh orange and lemonade but with something else

Richard could almost taste the sweet on his tongue as he read the description.  It really had been delicious!  If only he'd been able to bring some back with him!   It really wasn't fair! Suddenly, he heard Nilbog's voice.

"Look in the pocket of your jeans, Richard!" he said.  "There's a treat in there for you!" Nilbog appeared on the foot of the bed as Richard reached out for his jeans, and felt in the pockets. There was something there!  He pulled it out and looked at it.  It was a special, small, silvery bag. He felt inside the bag, and found ....... a sweet!  It was one of the magic sweets from Fantasy Land -

an orange one!  Richard could hardly believe it!
The orange ones were his favourites!

"But I thought you said I couldn't bring any home
with me!" he said, popping it quickly into his
mouth.

"That's right, you couldn't - but there's nothing to
stop me from bringing you some every now and
then!" Nilbog replied.  "Put the bag somewhere
safe, and look in it regularly.  Every now and then,
I'll put a treat in there for you, if I think you've
deserved it!"

"Thanks, Nilbog," Nilbog clicked his fingers and
disappeared as suddenly as he had appeared and
Richard settled down to read the rest of the
chapter, chewing on his magic sweet as he did so.

"Don't forget to brush your teeth again before you
go to sleep," Nilbog's voice reminded him. "Even
magic sweets are bad for your teeth, you know!"

"I won't.  I promise!"  Richard replied, "and a
promise is a promise, you know!"

# Chapter 16  I'm Shrinking

The next day was Saturday and the weather was beautiful - better than it had been for ages. It was one of those days when nearly all mothers say to their children, "What are you doing sitting in front of the television? It's far too nice a day to be inside. Go out and play in the garden! Get some fresh air - after all, it will probably rain tomorrow, and then you'll have to stay inside!" - and that is exactly what Richard's mother said to him, so out he had to go! There's no point in arguing when mothers say that sort of thing. We all know that they just won't listen to arguments. Mothers know best - or at least, they think they do!

Richard didn't really know what to do when he got outside, so he kicked a stone around for a while, then he found his basketball hiding behind one of the bushes, so he picked it up and aimed a few shots at his basketball hoop, but it wasn't much fun without someone to play with. He wandered over to his climbing frame and swing set and played on that for a little while, but he got bored with that as well. It isn't much fun being an only child when you need someone to play with, and there were times when Richard was well and truly fed up with being an only child!

Suddenly, a strange, tingly feeling came over him, and he realised that he was shrinking! He seemed to grow smaller and smaller until he was about a quarter of his usual size. "Nilbog!" he shouted. "Where are you? What's happening?"

"I'm here," came a small voice behind him.. Richard looked round, but could see nothing. "Look down, you twit!" the voice said. He looked down towards his feet, and saw that Nilbog had shrunk too, but he had shrunk even more. He was no taller than a mouse! "Are you ready for adventure number four? You'll need to shrink some more if you are. You're not small enough yet!"

"I ..... I suppose so!" Richard replied, "If you're sure we'll be all right!"

"I'm sure!" Nilbog replied. "I do this all the time!" He seemed to click his fingers again (although they were so small now that Richard couldn't really tell for certain!) and Richard continued to shrink, until he too was not much taller than a mouse! He looked around. Everything looked so different when you were tiny. Normal, everyday things like grass looked like a jungle, so thick that he could hardly see through it. He wouldn't have been a bit surprised to see a monkey swinging from branch to branch, or tigers skulking in the shadows! It made him feel a little nervous. Thank goodness Nilbog was with him, he thought. He looked up to see if he could see the sky above him but the flowers were absolutely huge. Even the daisies and dandelions towered above them both, hiding the sunlight like giant beach umbrellas. Suddenly, a bee flew down to get some pollen from one of the flowers. Richard felt rather nervous, it seemed so huge from his new, miniature height! He nudged Nilbog, and they ran to hide under a large dandelion leaf - just in case the bee decided that it wanted something more than pollen! A spider scampered past, all eight legs moving rapidly as it searched for more food. Richard had never seen a spider look so huge, and its legs were incredibly hairy - even hairier than his dads, Richard thought, mischievously!  He wondered what a tarantula might look like to someone as small as he was right now, and shivered at the thought!

When the bee had finally flown away and the spider had gone on its journey, Richard peeped out.  He couldn't see any dangers, so cautiously, carefully, he walked a bit further forwards and Nilbog followed close behind.  They pushed their way through the enormous blades of grass, deeper and deeper, further and further, until, suddenly they came to Richard's sand pit and gazed upon the beautiful sand castle that was there.

A couple of weeks earlier, Richard and one of his friends had been playing around in there.  They had tried using it as a long jump pit, practising for Sports Day; then they had got bored with jumping, had sat down in the sand and had built a wonderful sand-castle, complete with a moat and a drawbridge, and plastic soldiers to guard it.  They had got carried away with their design and had given it four, tall turrets, one at each corner, and had built an even taller tower in the middle. They had carved patterns into the walls, and decorated it with sticks and pebbles. They had even made a flag and had stuck it into the centre tower. It had looked quite impressive from above, when Richard had been his normal height, and they had been very proud of it. For once, they had not wanted to destroy it when Alex had to go home, and so they had left it, right in the centre of the sand pit, where it had remained ever since. Right now, it looked even more amazing! Very little rain had fallen over the last fortnight, so the design on the walls had not been washed away. The massive structure towered above Richard and Nilbog, its four turrets appearing so huge that they nearly touched the sky and its flag was still waving in the breeze. Next to it was a mountain of sand and rocks that Richard couldn't remember building, although he supposed he must have done at some stage! Perhaps it was some of the sand that he had dug out when he was building the moat. He was sure it would look nowhere near as huge when he next looked down at it from his normal height.  He looked proudly at his creation.

"Look at our castle, Nilbog!" said Richard, proudly. "I built that with Alex a couple of weeks ago when he came round to play, and it's still there! Doesn't it look super?  You'd almost expect royalty to be living inside it - apart from the fact that it's solid!"

"It's very good, but are you really sure it's solid?" Nilbog asked, leading the way across the drawbridge towards the large piece of wood that the boys had used as a front door.  Richard was astounded to see the great door open, almost as if by magic, and there, in front of him, was a huge, beautifully carved entrance hall, with an amazing stairway just ahead!

## Chapter 17   Inside the Sand Castle!

Richard looked around him in amazement.  He couldn't believe his eyes!

"We didn't give it an inside, Nilbog!" he gasped.  "We couldn't have done anything as marvellous as this!  It was hard enough trying to hollow out a tunnel under the drawbridge.  This must have been really difficult, so who could have done it?"

Nilbog gave his usual reply.  "Wait and see!" he said.

"You always say that!" Richard replied.  "You're as bad as Mum!"

"That's because I don't want to ruin the surprise," Nilbog replied.  Slowly, Richard walked a little further forward; gazing around as he did so, but then, suddenly, he heard a tiny voice coming from somewhere near his feet which made him stop in his tracks.

"Oy!  Watch where you're walking in our castle!" it squeaked.  "You nearly trod on me there, you great clumsy oaf!"  Richard looked down, and saw an ant standing by his feet, its tiny hands on its hips, looking at him bossily.  Even at his new, smaller size, the ant looked small to him. It barely came up to his ankles! "Who are you anyway," it continued, "and what are you doing in our castle? Oh - or did you come with Nilbog? Hello there, Nilbog! Welcome back! How do you like the improvements?"

"Hello, Tina!" Nilbog replied. "Yes, he's with me. I hope you don't mind. I thought he might like to see what you've done in here!"

"Did you say it was your castle?" Richard asked. "Did you make the inside?"

"Well, not by myself!" the small ant admitted. "You don't think I could do this all by myself, do you? Ants always work as a team. You'd be amazed what we can do when we set our minds to it!" The ant stopped to look at Richard. "Was it you who built the outside? I'm sure you're the one we watched - but you were much bigger then!"

"Yes," Richard agreed. "It was me - well me and my friend! My name's Richard. I live in the big house at the other end of the garden. You say you were watching us, but why?"

"Yes, we were.  You see, someone dug up our old home, so we had to find somewhere else to live. Lots of the older ants had been sent out on a search and I thought I'd follow, but I took a short cut through your garden and saw you building this, so I ran straight back to tell the other ants about it.  Of course, we all liked the idea of living in a castle, so we thought we'd give it a try."

"But, how did you hollow it out?" Richard asked.  It was solid when we left it!"

"We used our feet." Tina replied.  "It took ages and ages to carve out all the rooms, and we had to cart the sand away as we did it, but we all think it's worth it.  It's a lovely place to live!"

"So that's where the sand mountain came from!" Richard remarked.  "I didn't think I remembered building that!"

"We wouldn't normally move it so far," the ant replied, "but we didn't want to ruin the castle!  It's so nice!"

"Can I see some more of the rooms?" Richard asked.

"Of course - but we've still not quite finished them all yet.  If you look carefully, you'll see some of the other ants scurrying around, carting sand back outside."

They walked on through the entrance hall towards another doorway, this time quite a bit smaller. There was no way that Richard and Nilbog would be able to get through at their present height. "Hang on a minute, Tina!" Nilbog said.  "Richard, we're going to have to shrink a bit more if you want to continue exploring.  Are you ready for it?" "I suppose so!" Richard replied.  Once more, Nilbog clicked his fingers, and he felt the funny, tingly feeling all through his body once more as they shrank further, until they were only a little bit taller than Tina.
"OK Tina, we're ready!" Nilbog said, and once again they moved forwards into the room ahead. Richard was amazed to see that it was full of tiny, worm-like creatures, wriggling around! Some were eating food that had been brought in, whilst others looked to be sleeping.

"What is this room, Tina?" he asked. "What are all these creatures?"

"This is the nursery," she replied, "and these are my baby brothers and sisters. You see, ants are a bit like butterflies in the way we grow. Each Queen lays thousands of eggs at a time, and we hatch out as larvae, like this. They will change their skins several times, and eventually they will change totally and turn into ants."

"It's called metamorphosis," Nilbog added. "Frogs and toads do it as well in their own way, you know. They hatch out as tadpoles, and change totally to become frogs."

"Yes - we've seen that in school," Richard replied. "We had a tank of tadpoles in the classroom last year, and I knew about caterpillars of course, but I didn't know ants did the same sort of thing! Do many other animals change like that?"

"Quite a lot of different insects do," Tina replied. "You'll have to look it up. Some of these baby ants will grow up to be soldier ants like me; some will be hunters, and will go to get the food; and some will help to look after the Queens and the young ants.  It is possible that one of them may grow up to be a Queen herself!"

"Insects are interesting in the ways they grow," Nilbog added.  "Some insects change in different ways, like Dragonflies and Mayflies.  I'm sure you'll be able to find out more if you want."

"I suppose so!" Richard replied.  "I'd like to know more about it!  How many ants live in this castle, Tina?"

"Only about fifty or sixty thousand," came the reply.  "But I'm not sure exactly how many there are.  I've never counted!"

"*Only* about fifty or sixty thousand?" Richard gasped.  "*Really*?  You mean *fifty thousand* ants can live in my sand-castle!  Crumbs!"  He could hardly believe what he heard.  It sounded like a really huge number.

"Yes, but it could be more.  As I say, I'm really not sure.  Ants always live together in very large groups.  It's rather like what you humans call a city. We all work together to make sure that everything runs smoothly."

"Do you all have special jobs?" Richard asked.

"Oh yes," Tina replied. "We have to, otherwise nothing would get done! I'm a soldier ant. It's my job to guard the castle and to protect the Queens and all the other ants from danger." She looked at Richard. "Don't you humans all have special jobs and tasks?"

"I suppose we do!" Richard agreed. "I have my chores - but I don't always want to do them! Some of them are really boring!"

"But if you didn't do them, it would cause problems for your family, wouldn't it?" Tina asked.

"Yes, I suppose it would. Someone would have to do them, anyway, and they wouldn't be very happy about it!"

"Quite!" Nilbog added.

"Do you want to see a bit more?" Tina asked

"Yes please!" Richard replied eagerly. The moved towards the next room, but Tina suddenly stopped near the door.

"You must be really quiet if you want to look in this room," she said. "This is the room where one of the Queens lives. She lays her eggs in here, and when they hatch they move into the nursery."

They peeped round the door.  Richard was horrified to see a huge ant surrounded by what looked like thousands of tiny, white eggs.

He gasped in amazement.  "Crikey!"

"Ssshhhh!" Tina said, pulling him out.

"But, however many eggs are there?"

"I'm not sure," she replied.  "There's probably nearly twenty thousand.  That's how many she usually lays."

"Twenty thousand!"  Richard gasped. "Good grief! That's a huge number! Do you mean all those eggs will hatch into ants?"

"Not all of them, but eventually many of them will and there are three other Queens in this castle, all laying eggs.  Now you know why there are so many ants around!" Nilbog replied.

"But we have to keep reproducing like this," Tina added.  "There are so many dangers out there for us to face every day.   Animals and birds want to eat us all the time.  They reckon we taste nice! Humans stand on us because they aren't looking where they are going, and some even set traps for us, or try to destroy our nests because they think we're dirty and they want rid of us. Millions of ants are killed every day, and nobody gives it a thought."

"That sounds awful, Tina!" Richard said, horrified.

"Think about it.  You nearly trod on me a little while back because you weren't looking where you were going!"

"I suppose I did," Richard admitted.  "I'm sorry.  I'll try to be more careful in future."

"Also, you have to remember that only the Queen can lay eggs.  The rest of us can't have babies at all.  She lays the eggs for all the ants in the castle."

"Right.  When you put it like that, it doesn't sound so many!"  Richard thought for a moment.  "Tina, I've sometimes watched the ants in the garden. They all seem to be following some kind of a trail, forwards and backwards - like they were playing 'Follow my Leader'.  What are they doing?"

"They're following the smell.  When a hunter ant finds a good supply of food, it lays an invisible scent trail on the ground, leading back to the nest.  Other hunter ants follow the trail so that

they can find the food easily, and we guard them."
She looked accusingly at Richard and continued.
"Sometimes, of course, people try to confuse us
by putting something in the way, then we soldier
ants have to try and find their way round it and to
lay a new trail for the others to follow.  It can be
quite dangerous, but it's the only way any of us
can get home!"  She paused, and looked around,
while Richard felt himself go slightly red.  That
was a game he had played more than once, and
now he had a bit of a guilty conscience about it!
Perhaps it was a rather unkind trick to play after
all - but it had seemed like harmless fun at the
time.

"Anyway, it's been nice meeting you, Richard, but
I'm going to have to go and get on with my work.
There's always a lot to do in an ants nest - even if
it is a castle like this!  I can't stand around here
gossiping all day when there's work to be done.
I'm sure you can see yourselves out!  Goodbye,
both of you!"  She scurried off rapidly, leaving
Richard and Nilbog watching.  Richard was
amazed at the speed she ran!

"I wish I could run like that!" he remarked.

"I know.  They're quite amazing," Nilbog remarked.  "Did you know, ants are incredible athletes!  If they were the same size as humans, they would win the running races and the weight lifting classes in the Olympic games."

"Really?"

"Yes. Because they have such long legs, they are amazing sprinters, and they carry really heavy things for their size!  You've seen some of the things they carry from place to place.  They are a lot heavier than the ant who is carrying it!"

Richard was amazed.

"I shall certainly look at ants differently after this adventure!" he retorted.

Richard and Nilbog made their way out of the castle and headed towards the sand mountain.

"Do you want to look at the view from the top, Richard?" Nilbog asked.

"Might be fun!" Richard replied.

"Easy way, or hard way?"

"Oh, easy I think!" Richard replied, lazily.  Nilbog clicked his fingers, and they both grew back to mouse height; then he clicked them again, and they both found themselves perched on the very top of the sand mountain.

## Chapter 18    In the garden

Richard gazed out at the view beyond him.  The
sand pit looked almost like a desert, with the
castle rising up out of it.  Beyond it was the
'jungle' of grass that they had pushed their way
through earlier.  Further on, they could see what
looked like a lake (which was really the garden
pond) where monstrous fish would be swimming,
and huge frogs jumping and splashing, and way in
the distance, they could see Richard's house.
They sat and looked for a while; then Richard
suddenly thought of something, and giggled.

"What is it?" Nilbog asked.

"Oh I've just thought of some jokes Grandad told
me last weekend about ants.  They were quite
funny!" Richard replied

"Oh, what were they?"

"What is the largest ant in the world?" Richard
asked.

"I don't know," Nilbog replied.  "What is the
largest ant in the world?"

"A gi - ant!" They both laughed.

"And do you know when an ant carries a trunk?" Nilbog asked

"No idea!  When does an ant carry a trunk?" Richard replied.

"When it's an eleph - ant!"

"I've got a knock, knock joke as well," Richard added.

"Go on then," Nilbog replied.  "I'm ready!"

"Knock, knock!"

"Who's there?"

"Ant"

"Ant who?"

"Ant you ever going to open this door and let me in!"  They both laughed again, then Nilbog turned to Richard.

"Do you like sledging?" he asked.

"Yes, I love it," Richard replied.  "Why?"

"Do you fancy sledging down this hill?"

"It would be brilliant," Richard replied, "but surely you can only sledge in Winter?  You need snow, and we haven't got any!"

"No, but we've got plenty of sand all ready and waiting!" Nilbog replied. "Have you never tried sand sledging?"

"No, I haven't, but it sounds like fun!" Richard paused for a moment. "There's just one problem. We haven't got a sledge!"

"No problem," Nilbog replied, and he clicked his fingers. Suddenly, there in front of them was the most beautiful, shiny, silver and blue sledge that Richard had ever seen. "On you get!" Nilbog remarked, jumping onto the sledge himself. "I'll go at the front, because I know what I'm doing. You sit behind me, and hold on tight!"

Richard jumped onto the sledge behind Nilbog, and put his arms around the elf's waist. "Let's go!" he shouted, and they were off, very slowly at first, but getting faster and faster as the slope got steeper. Sand sledging was amazing! Richard could feel the wind on his face and in his hair, and he couldn't stop himself from shouting out in delight as the sledge got faster. "Woohay!"

Soon they were whizzing down the slope! It was fantastic, in fact, if anything sand sledging was even better than sledging on the snow, because it wasn't as cold (although it was a little bumpy in places!)  This was far more exciting even than the huge water flumes they'd been on in the holidays! Part of him wanted to close his eyes, but part of him didn't dare; just in case they crashed into something and he fell off!  He let out another shriek of delight.

As they neared the bottom, the slope got less steep, and the sledge started to slow down. Richard was a little concerned that it wasn't slowing down quickly enough.  The wooden edge of the sand pit was getting closer and closer. Surely they were going to crash!  He held on to Nilbog even tighter.  The sledge slowed some more, then a little more until it came to a stop just short of the edge.

"Phew!" Richard exclaimed with relief.

"What do you mean, phew!" Nilbog demanded.

"You didn't think I was going to let you crash, did you?"

"Well, we did seem to be going a bit fast," Richard admitted, "but I suppose I knew that we were safe really!"

"Of course we were!" Nilbog replied. Suddenly, they heard Richard's mother calling to him.

"Ooops! I'm going to have to go in!" Richard remarked. "It must be tea time!"

"What, like that?" Nilbog asked. "Don't you want me to do something first?"

Richard looked down and giggled. "Well, yes! It might give her a bit of a shock! Perhaps it might be an idea if you could un-shrink me first, please!"

Nilbog clicked his fingers, and Richard felt the strange, tingly feeling spread all over his body again, as he slowly grew back to his normal height.

What they hadn't realised was that Richard's next-door neighbour's large, black and white cat had been sitting, watching them and plotting! It quite fancied the idea of two, mouse-sized people for tea, and was just ready to pounce! Imagine its shock and surprise when its 'tea' magically grew under its very eyes - and it realised that what it had been about to eat was now a full sized Richard!  His fur stood on end in fear, his back arched and he hissed at them.  Nilbog pointed his finger straight at the cat, and it turned and fled in a panic, running away so quickly that it couldn't see where he was going - straight into the middle of the pond!  Although he knew he shouldn't, Richard couldn't help laughing at the sight of the rather soggy cat, sitting amongst the piles of pond weed in the pond!  Pond weed was dangling over its face, and as they watched, a small frog jumped off the poor cat's ear, making Richard laugh even more.

"Thanks, Nilbog.  It's been fun!" Richard said, turning around to see him; but Nilbog had vanished already.  "I can't wait to read about it all tonight!"

"Good for you," Nilbog's voice answered him, as if from nowhere.  "You're getting there!"

"I guess I am," Richard replied, as he ran in to wash his hands.

## Chapter 19   The book again.

"I think that wretched cat has been fishing in our pond again!" Dad remarked during tea. "I saw him disappear over the fence, looking rather wet and bedraggled.  If he fell in this time, maybe he'll learn!  I'm fed up with losing my prize fish to that moggy!"

Richard smiled as he remembered the sight of the poor, soggy creature. "He did fall in.  I saw him in the pond," he admitted.  "He did look a sight!"

His father smiled. "I guess that's what you might call a rather soggy moggy!" he laughed.  Richard laughed too, but Mum wasn't so sure.

"I hope you didn't chase him, Richard.  We don't want Mr Smith coming to complain that we've been terrorising his cat!" Mum commented.

"No, I didn't," Richard replied.  "It's not nice to chase animals - even if they are as nasty and cruel as that cat, but he did look funny!"

"I bet he did!  And I wouldn't worry about terrorising cats!  Look at the number of times he's terrorised my fish over the years!" Dad was not at all fond of cats, particularly when they were fishing in his pond!  Richard told his parents about the frog jumping off the cat's ear, and they all laughed!

"I wish I'd seen it!" Dad smiled.

After tea that night, Richard didn't even wait to see what was on the television.  It could have been all his favourite programmes, or absolutely nothing he liked for all he cared.  He just HAD to get upstairs and read his book!  That adventure had been such fun; he had to read what Nilbog had written about it!  He charged into his bedroom and yanked his book out of his bag, then he threw himself onto his bed and settled down to read the next chapter, but first of all, he slid his hand under his pillow to find his magic, silvery bag.  Would Nilbog have put anything in there for him tonight?  Carefully, he pulled the magic bag out and opened it. To his delight, there was not one, but three of the magic sweets in there! He took one out - a pink one - and slipped it into his mouth, letting the delicious raspberry flavour explode onto his tongue. It was just as magical as he had remembered! Next, he opened the book and found the new chapter.

## Chapter 9

The next day, the weather was beautiful - better than it had been for ages. It was one of those days when nearly all mothers say to their children, "What are you doing sitting in front of the television? It's far too nice a day to be inside. Go out and play in the garden! Get some fresh air - after all, it will probably rain tomorrow, and then you'll have to stay inside!" - and that is exactly what Richard's mother said to him, so out he had to go! There's no point in arguing when mothers say that sort of thing. We all know that they just won't listen to us. Mothers know best! (At least, they think they do!) Richard didn't know what to do when he got outside, so he kicked a stone around for a little while, then he found his basketball hiding in one of the bushes, so he picked it up and aimed a few shots at his basketball hoop, but it wasn't much fun without someone to play with.

Suddenly, a strange, tingly feeling came all over him, and he realised that he was shrinking!

Richard remembered that feeling very strongly. It was like nothing he had ever felt before, and the way everything around him had seemed to grow - until he realised that it wasn't everything growing; it was him shrinking!

He pulled another of the magical sweets out of his silver bag - a green one this time, and turned the page, ready to continue reading. It was nearly as exciting reading about his adventures like this as it had been when he had experienced them. If he felt like this, perhaps other people would enjoy reading his book as well. Richard was beginning to realise that, perhaps, one of the things that he would have to do with this book was to pass it on, and let other people read about what he'd done and where he'd been - but somehow he knew that he would never be able to tell anyone that they were true!  After all, no-one would believe him - unless, of course, they'd had a magic book of their own at some time!  Never mind!  He knew it was true - and he still had one more adventure to look forwards to!

## Chapter 20   Ergo

It was Sunday morning, and Richard had been enjoying a lie in.  It was nice to know that he didn't have to hurry to get up for school, and that no-one would be shouting at him and saying, "Hurry up, or you'll be late!"  He picked up his magic book, and looked at it longingly.  Although part of him couldn't wait for the next adventure, part of him didn't want it to come too soon, because he knew that it would mean an end to all this fun.

He flicked through a few pages, then, all of a sudden, he came across a picture near the back of the book - one that he had never noticed before.  He looked at it carefully.  It looked like a cottage with a beautiful garden.  Nearby, there were woods, and somebody had left an axe near one of the trees.  As Richard looked at the picture, he started to wonder who might live there.  Could it be a nice family, or a prince, hiding from danger?  Could it be an evil witch, or could it be a fairy tale cottage of some sort?  Could it be something to do with his next adventure?  He looked a little closer, trying to find a clue; but as he did so, to his amazement he was convinced that he saw the door open up in front of him, and someone start to come out.

As he looked more closely at the picture, suddenly everything went all misty and swimmy in front of him, and he felt himself being pulled straight into the picture!  It felt very peculiar, and Richard found that he just had to close his eyes.  When the swimmy feeling stopped, he opened them again and found himself standing on the path in front of the largest 'cottage' that he had ever seen.  It was absolutely enormous!  The door was nearly as tall as his own house, and the flowers growing below the windows were taller than him! Naturally, his first thought was "Oh, no!  I've shrunk again!" He looked around a bit more, then he heard Nilbog behind somewhere him, calling his name.

"Richard!  So there you are at last!  What took you so long!  I've been waiting ages!" Nilbog said.

Richard turned around to reply, but found himself staring at ... the hugest, hairiest pair of shins he had ever seen!  He looked up, past a huge pair of hairy knees, some even huger, hairier thighs, an enormous pair of green shorts, a bright red shirt which was partly open to reveal a very hairy chest, and the hairy, red, bearded face of ... a giant!

"Wh ...who are you?" Richard stammered nervously.  "Wh ... where am I, and where's Nilbog?"

"I'm here, you twit!   On his shoulder!" Nilbog replied.  Richard looked again, and saw Nilbog perched there, high up.  "This is Ergo.  He's ever so friendly.  He offered to give me a ride!  So what caused your delay?  Couldn't you find the picture, or were you being lazy!"

"Both, I guess!" Richard replied.  "But it is Saturday!  Saturday is lazy day in my house!  Hello, Ergo.  It's good to meet you!"

"**Good to meet you, Richard. Do you want a ride as well?**" the giant boomed in an extremely loud voice, shaking everything around him and making Richard jump. "**There's room for both of you up here.**" He bent down, and Richard clambered up. It was a bit like climbing a tree! First he pulled himself up onto the giant's huge knee; then he clambered his way up his arms and onto the shoulder. When Richard was in place, the Giant slowly stood up. It felt a bit wobbly as he did so, but once he was upright, the view from his shoulders was amazing. They could see for miles and miles and there were so many wonderful things to see! Houses and castles, animals, trees, - loads of things. It was a bit like being in a hot air balloon!

"Where are we going, Nilbog?" Richard asked.

"**To my house,**" Ergo replied, very loudly. He didn't seem capable of using a quiet voice. "**I live at the other side of these woods. That was my Grandmother's cottage that you landed at. I** visit her every day to take her a meal. She's very old now, so she doesn't cook for herself any more, but I always make enough for her as well as for me."

"That's kind of you." Richard said. "How old is your grandmother?"

**"She was 185 last week,"** Ergo replied. **"That's quite old for a giant."**

"It would be very old for a human, too," Richard remarked. "I don't think any human has ever lived that long! Even my Great-Gran is only 80, I think!"

"It's still quite young for an elf," Nilbog commented. "I was 150 a couple of weeks ago!"

Richard looked at him in amazement. "But you still look really young!" he gasped. "I thought you were only about the same age as my teacher!"

"Elves can live up to six hundred years, so in elf terms I am still quite young!" Nilbog replied.

"I suppose you are!" Richard replied.

Ergo loped along, each huge stride taking them further and further into the woods.  It seemed strange to be so high up!  He could look straight into the birds' nests, and watch the baby birds chirping and opening their greedy mouths to demand more food.  The parent birds flew past his face, with worms in their beaks ready to feed the chicks.  It was incredible to be at the same height and to be able to see so much.

Before long, they reached the end of the woods, and there in front of them was another huge, but beautifully welcoming cottage.  Its walls were white but it had a red, pointed roof, a light green, wooden door and light green window frames.  The garden was full of flowers, and there were roses of all colours growing up the windows.  It really did look lovely.

**"Here we are, home safely!"** Ergo boomed, as he opened the front door and carried Nilbog and

Richard through to the kitchen - a large, spacious room with an enormous, wooden table and four gigantic chairs in the middle. As Richard looked around, he could see a large, wooden dresser against one wall, and a very old fashioned cooker on another wall. Otherwise, the room looked very bare. **"Now, I could do with a drink after that walk. I'm a bit thirsty."** Ergo boomed. **"Does anyone else want one?"**

"Yes please," Richard replied. "I'd love one, please, Ergo. I'm thirsty too. Nilbog's picture found me before I'd managed to have any breakfast!"

The giant placed Richard and Nilbog down on the table and wandered over to the enormous sink to find a glass. It was the largest glass that Richard had ever seen - it looked more like a large, glass bucket, but the water looked fresh and clear. Ergo filled it with water and brought it over to where they were standing. Richard and Nilbog looked at it in amazement. Thirsty as they were, there was no way that either of them would be able to pick it up and drink out of it!  But Ergo didn't see the looks on their faces, and he went back to pour himself an equally large glass of water, which he drank very quickly.  He looked at Richard and Nilbog.

**"You're not drinking!"** he shouted, in amazement.  **"Aren't you thirsty?"**

Richard and Nilbog looked at one another.  Could he really not see what the problem was?  Perhaps he really wasn't a very clever giant after all!  "Yes!" Richard said, finally. "I'm very thirsty, but this glass is going to be really hard for us to drink out of, Ergo.  It's so big and heavy.  We can't pick it up!  Do you have anything smaller that we could drink out of?"

**"I might have something,"** Ergo replied.  **"I've got some thimbles in my bedroom that I use when I'm mending my clothes.  Perhaps they would be a better size for you.  I'll just go**

**look!"** He walked out of the room into the hallway, and as he went, Richard could feel everything shake. A little water spilt over the top of the glass. He looked around to see if there was a cloth or something to mop up the spill. He was in luck! Over at the other side of the table, he could see a huge recipe book, and next to it there was an enormous paper towel! He ran over and tore a bit off the paper towel, and as he did so, he couldn't help but read the page that the book was open on.

In enormous writing, just in front of him was the title of a recipe for ... Little Boy Pie with Green Goblin Sauce!

Richard gasped in horror! All this time he had thought that Ergo was nice, all the nice things he had done, and now this! He and Nilbog were in danger - BIG DANGER! They had to do something quickly, or this would be an adventure that he would not be able to escape from! Quickly, he ran back to the water glass. It would not do for Ergo to find out that he had discovered the Giant's secret, but in the meantime, he had to tell Nilbog what was going on!

## Chapter 21   Danger!

Quickly, he ran back across the table to where Nilbog was waiting. "We've got problems," he whispered, and he told Nilbog what he'd seen. "We've got to get out of here quickly!" he added. Nilbog clicked his fingers but, to their great horror, nothing happened.

"We've got even more problems," he muttered back. "My magic isn't working either! I think something must be blocking it!"

"Try again!" Richard replied, so Nilbog clicked his fingers once more. Perhaps he hadn't clicked them firmly enough, or something; but still nothing happened. He looked at Richard, panic on his face.
"What do we do now?" Richard asked, beginning to panic.

"I don't know!" Nilbog replied. "We'll have to think about it!"

They thought about it for a minute or so, then suddenly they realised that they could both feel and hear the giant coming back. He was carrying two enormous thimbles - but at least they were smaller and more manageable than the huge bucket sized glass that he'd given them before. He was also carrying what must have been the largest banana in the world! It was easily as large as Richard!

**"Will these do?"** Ergo shouted, pouring a small amount of water into them from the glass, and handing them carefully to Richard and Nilbog. Although the tops looked quite thick, they were certainly a much better size for them to drink out of.

"That's great. Err, thanks, Ergo!" Richard replied, trying very hard to breathe normally, but still panicking inside. How were they going to get out of this one?

Ergo opened the banana, and broke a small piece off, which he offered to Richard. **"You said you hadn't had any breakfast,"** he boomed. **"Would you like some banana?"** Richard was feeling really puzzled now. The giant still seemed to be really friendly, but it didn't fit with what he'd just seen in the recipe book. How could someone be so friendly, and yet so ferocious as to be planning to cook them and eat them for dinner? But then again, what was blocking Nilbog's magic? It had worked earlier, to bring them to Giant land, so why wasn't it working now? Perhaps the giant was waiting until he and Nilbog were separated before beginning his plan. Perhaps he was trying to fatten them up, to make a better sized meal. Perhaps he was having second thoughts. Whatever it was, Richard was convinced that they would have to act quickly! He had to think of something before it was too late!

He took a few sips of the water and nibbled on the piece of banana that Nilbog had given him, and began to feel a bit calmer. Surely Nilbog and he could come up with some sort of plan - after all, they had managed to defeat the shark between them.  Surely this couldn't be a lot worse!  He sipped a bit more, and as he did so, an idea came to his mind.  He remembered the trick he had played on his father on April Fool's Day, when he had tied Dad's shoe laces together.  Perhaps that would work; after all, the Giant was wearing huge, lace-up boots.

Richard remembered that it had been very funny at the time.   When Dad stood up to walk, he had fallen all over the place!  (Well, Richard and his Mum had thought it was funny, even if his Dad hadn't!)  If he could do the same thing to the giant, perhaps it would stop him from chasing them while they made their escape!  Perhaps it would slow him down just enough for them to get far enough away from the cottage for Nilbog's magic to work again!   He took a few more sips of water and tried to think his idea through a bit more.  Perhaps that was what they would have to do!

He looked up at the huge Giant, who was holding yet another rather large piece of banana out for him. "Thanks, Ergo," he said, taking it from the enormous, hairy hand. It would be rude to refuse his kind offer, and he was beginning to feel very hungry - even if he didn't want to think about hunger right now. When he'd finally had enough water and had eaten his piece of banana, he handed the thimble back to Ergo, who took it over to the sink. While his back was turned, Richard looked over at Nilbog. The idea was nearly fully formed in his mind. "We've got to get him sitting down somehow, Nilbog!" Richard muttered, very quietly. "I've got to be able to get at his shoelaces, so you'll have to distract him somehow. Think hard!"

"I'll see if I can get him talking," Nilbog muttered back. "That should distract him for a while. You see if you can get off the table without him seeing you!"

"No, I've got a better idea!" Richard whispered back. "I've just thought of it." He turned to the giant. "Do you want to play a game? Have you ever played Hide and Seek?" he asked.

**"No,"** Ergo bellowed back, dropping the banana skin onto the table next to where Nilbog was standing. **"How do you play it?"**

Richard explained the rules of the game, and the giant shut his eyes and started counting to 50. While he was counting, Richard climbed down from the table onto one of the huge chairs. From there, it was possible to slide carefully down to the floor. He then crept around the giant's huge right foot and grabbed the shoelace. Giving it a gentle yank, he reached out and grabbed the left shoelace in his other hand. They were so thick, it was like holding two ropes together! Very, very carefully, he tied them both together in a huge knot, and then he left them on the floor and darted off to hide behind the enormous table leg.

The giant continued counting - but he wasn't very good at maths and really didn't know his numbers very well at all, so he kept getting stuck. After he had reached 'twenty' for the third time, missing out one or two numbers on the way every time and could still not get any further, Richard decided to take the risk and get him moving.

"Come and find me, Ergo!" Richard shouted in a friendly way, pretending to be playing still. The giant stood up to get him, but as he tried to move his feet, he found that they wouldn't go far enough. He tried again, confused as to what was happening, and found himself starting to fall. He reached out to stop himself, but fell back onto the chair with a mighty crack - which broke it clean in two, and he landed on his bottom flat on the floor. As anyone who has fallen out of a chair knows, it hurts a lot when you do that, and the giant's cried out in pain.

**"Ow! My bottom!"** he shouted, very loudly. **"That hurt!"** He tried to get up again, but somehow managed to bang his elbow on the table leg, then, seconds later, he knocked his head on the bottom of the table as he tried to get up for a third time, making everything wobble as if they were in an earthquake. The glasses fell off the table and smashed onto the floor. He reached out his hand towards the dresser, and pulled it over as he fell once more. Bowls and plates crashed down all around the poor giant, creating a cacophony of sound all around. Slowly, painfully, he eased his way back up onto his feet and tried to take another step forwards, but he was going nowhere quickly.

Next, Nilbog threw the gigantic banana skin down from the table. Richard caught it, and ran round behind the giant. He carefully slid it under the giant's foot, just underneath the spot where he was going to step. His foot was now hovering centimetres above it. In a matter of seconds, foot and banana skin would meet, and the inevitable would happen. Richard and Nilbog watched, scarcely able to breathe. Would the giant's foot and the banana skin meet?  Would it work?   The giant wibbled and wobbled for a second or two, then suddenly his foot wobbled once more and came down, straight onto the banana skin.  Once again, the giant found himself flat on his back on the floor!  He started to cry, and the noise was like nothing that Richard or Nilbog had ever heard before.

**"It's not fair!"**  he howled.  **"I thought you were my friends, but you're being horrible to me and I don't like it.  Why are you picking on me like this, and what have you done to my shoes?"** He sat on the floor looking very miserable.

"You wanted to eat us!" Richard replied.  "We didn't like that either.  We had to try and stop you!  We didn't want to be eaten!"

**"I didn't want to eat you!   What makes you think that I want to eat you?"** Ergo replied. **"I don't eat people.  I might be a giant, but I'm not an ogre and I've never eaten people.  None of my family do.  I just wanted to be your friend,**

and now you're being nasty to me. Boo hoo hoo!" The giant sobbed and sobbed, so much so that Richard really started to feel sorry for him. Perhaps they had misunderstood him? He seemed to be genuinely upset. Gigantic tears rolled down his cheeks and splashed onto the floor in huge puddles.

"Don't cry, Ergo," he said, paddling over to the giant through the huge puddles of tear-water and patting his large, hairy hand.

**"Why did you think I wanted to eat you?"** Ergo asked, a little calmer now. **"I wouldn't do that. You're my friends, and friends don't eat each other. Surely you know that?"**

"Richard saw your recipe book," Nilbog said. "It was open at a recipe for Little Boy Pie with Green Goblin Sauce. How do you explain that? And then my magic wouldn't work when I tried it, so we couldn't do anything. We were very worried! We thought you were planning something really nasty! We had to try to escape!"

**"But I didn't open it at that recipe,"** Ergo sobbed. **"I'd forgotten that it was even in the recipe book! It's one that I picked up at the Giant's Bookshop ages ago. It has a lovely recipe in it for Whole Roast Lamb with Oven Roast Vegetables. My friend is coming for dinner tonight, and I wanted to cook her something special! I thought that sounded nice!"** He looked up at them, gigantic tears still in his eyes. **"I can even show you the lamb now if you don't believe me. It's sitting in the fridge, all ready for cooking!"** he paused for a little while and tried to bite back his sobs, drying his tears on his huge sleeves, while Richard and Nilbog looked at each other in confusion, then he went on.

**"Anyway, no magic works in our houses. We Giants aren't allowed to use magic. It's been banned. Some people tried to carry on after the ban, and so the chief wizard put a blocking spell on all giants houses years and years ago.**

I thought you would know that, Nilbog!  When you go outside, your magic will work again!"

Guiltily, but still feeling rather puzzled, Richard climbed back onto the table to have another look at the recipe book and he couldn't believe his eyes when he saw it properly!

| Little Boy Pie with Green Goblin Sauce. | Whole Roast Lamb with Oven Roast Vegetables. |
|---|---|
| Ingredients:- 1 little boy<br>     1 green goblin<br>     10 onions - finely chopped<br>     Butter<br>     Vegetables to taste<br>     Pastry<br>     Milk<br>     Finely chopped parsley<br>Method<br>1) Fry the onions in butter until brown.<br>2) Add the little boy, and cook until he stops screaming<br>3) Add vegetables to taste.<br>4) Transfer to baking dish and cover with pastry.<br>5) Meanwhile, boil the green goblin in the milk until he stops calling you rude names.  Cut him up into tiny pieces and throw him back into the sauce.<br>6) Add chopped parsley and serve over the pie with plenty of mashed potatoes. | Ingredients:-  1 lamb without wool (if Little Bo-Peep will let you  have one)<br>          10 onions<br>          Vegetables to taste.<br><br>Method<br>1) Fry the onions in butter until brown.<br>2) Skin the lamb and add it to the onions.<br>3) Cook in a large oven for several hours.<br>4) For the last hour, add as many vegetables as you think you can eat, spreading them around the meat.<br>5) Serve the two together with plenty of roast potatoes. |

When he came back over and looked over the edge of the table, his face was rather red and he was looking very embarrassed.

"Ooops, Nilbog! I made a huge mistake!" he confessed. "I've just seen - I didn't read the book carefully enough. I only read one side. I didn't think to look at the opposite page." He paused, and looked at them both. "I'm so sorry. As soon as I saw the recipe for Little Boy Pie with Green Goblin Sauce, I panicked, but Ergo's right. The recipe for Whole Roast Lamb is on the same page! Would you believe it?" He turned shamefacedly to look at the giant. "Ergo, I'm really sorry! I can't believe that I thought you wanted to eat us! Can you forgive me?"

**"Will you be my friend now?"** the giant asked.

"Of course!" Richard assured him. "If you promise that you'll never try to eat us!"

**"Of course I promise! That's an easy promise to make! I told you that I don't eat people!"** Ergo replied. **"Can we play that game now? I like games!"**

"Yes, but just wait till I've untied your shoelaces!" Richard smiled, "then we can go outside and play."

# Chapter 22  A real Game of Hide and Seek

When they got outside, the first thing that Nilbog did was test his magic.  He clicked his fingers once, and straight away he became invisible.

"That's cheating, Nilbog!" Richard teased.  "You can't hide like that.  We'd never be able to find you - unless we trod on you by accident, and you wouldn't like that!"  There was another little click, and Nilbog reappeared in front of them.

"Just testing!" he said.  "I'm pleased to report that it still works.  Now, how about this game.  I'll be on - you two go and hide - but don't go out of the garden!"

"We won't!  We don't need to - the garden is big enough!" Richard agreed.  Nilbog closed his eyes and started to count, and Richard and the Giant moved away to hide.  The huge garden was a lovely place for a game of hide and seek - there were so many terrific places, especially for a boy of Richard's size!  He tried hiding behind a rose bush, but the prickles were like huge daggers, and they looked rather dangerous. Richard felt more than a little nervous of them, so he moved away quickly and ducked down behind a smaller, less dangerous looking plant. He looked up. Ergo was still searching for somewhere to hide, then suddenly he darted behind the shed - just in time. "Coming, ready or not!" Nilbog called. Richard stayed as still as he could and waited to be found.

They had a wonderful morning playing hide and seek and lots of other games. Not only were there lots of places where Richard could hide, it seemed that the Giant could find a lot of different hidey holes as well, and more than once they had trouble finding him! As the time went on, it became clear that Ergo really was a very friendly giant, and they began to wonder how they could ever have believed anything else about him. He lifted Richard up into one of the trees so that he could hide up there, and Nilbog had to cheat and use his magic to find him!

Eventually, however, all good things have to come to an end, and Richard and Nilbog had to return home. Ergo was very sad to see them both go, and tears fell down his cheeks once again.

**"Will you ever come back and see me?"** he sobbed.

"I really don't know, Ergo," Richard had to reply. "I'd like to - but this was the last of my magic adventures, so I don't know if I will ever be able to!"

"You'll just have to wait and see!" Nilbog told them, "but it really is time to go home now."

He clicked his fingers once again, and the misty, swimmy feeling came over Richard. When it had cleared, he found he was sitting on his bed once more, staring at the picture in his book - but the picture had changed! It now showed Ergo's cottage, not his grandmothers - and, in the middle of the garden was Ergo. As Richard looked, he was sure he could see the giant smile and give him a little wave!  He waved back, unsure if the giant could see him - still it was worth a try!

"Is this it, Nilbog?  Is this really goodbye?" Richard asked, sadly, looking up at his friend.  "Will I really never see you again?"

"You never know, Richard.  Keep looking, and you may find me, hiding somewhere else.  After all, you never can tell, can you!  There are lots of surprises, just waiting for us around the corner; and never is a very long time!"  He winked a sparkly green eye, clicked his fingers, and vanished for the last time.  Richard sat there, sadly for a while until he heard his mother's voice, calling to him to come downstairs for lunch.

## Chapter 23   Is this the end?

Somehow, Richard wasn't feeling as desperate to read this adventure as he had been with the last couple.  Not because he hadn't enjoyed himself, because he certainly had; but because he knew that it would be the last one.  He might never see Nilbog again now - but it had been wonderful while it lasted.  Slowly, he walked upstairs and pulled the book out of his bag.  Slowly, he turned to the next chapter to start reading about his adventure in Giant Land, and his meeting with Ergo.  He reached under the pillow. Would the magic silver bag of sweets still be there, or had it disappeared with Nilbog, back to where it came? He felt around.  Phew!  There it was - and it had three more sweets in it!  Proof that Nilbog still cared!  Richard pulled one out and sucked on it, letting the flavours melt on his tongue.  It was orange -  one of his favourites!  Then he settled back to read some more.

Before long, he was engrossed. He just didn't want to put the book down. His final adventure with Nilbog had been just as much fun as all the others, and it was great to read about it all. He remembered that peculiar, misty, swimmy feeling as he had almost fallen into the book. He turned the pages rapidly, reading every word greedily, enjoying reliving all the scary bits, as well as the funny bits. Nilbog's description of the giant falling over and sending everything flying was so funny, he laughed and laughed; then eventually he turned the final page and read the last, sad words:

# The End

Miserably, Richard closed the book. He was close to tears. He knew that the words "The End" really were final. There were no more adventures left for him in this book. He could hold onto it, and read his adventures over and over again, or he could take it back to Mr James and let him pass it on to someone else. Perhaps it would just be a book to them - after all, Nilbog had said that the magic was only for him, but hopefully they would enjoy it all the same. Whatever happened, he was certain that, for him, it was it was a very special book; one he would never forget! Perhaps he would never find another one like it - but he was determined to try! After all, one of the many things that Nilbog had taught him over the last week or so was the fact that reading could actually be fun!

He slid the book slowly, almost reluctantly, into his reading folder and lay back on his bed, closing his eyes. Dreams were not long coming - after all, he had so many wonderful adventures to remember and to think about!

## Chapter 24  Back at School

On Monday morning at school, when the bell went for break time, Richard did not rush out to play with the others as he normally would have done. Instead, he quietly slid the book out of his backpack and took it over to his teacher.

"Finished it already, Richard?" asked Mr James. "What did you think of it?"  Richard's eyes flashed. Did his teacher know the secret of the book? Could he possibly know what had happened last week?   He couldn't tell, but never mind, whether he did or didn't, there was only one reply that Richard could possibly give!

"It was … magic, sir!" he replied  "Are there any more like it?"

"I'm not sure, Richard," replied the teacher. "You'll have to read a few and see!"

"I will, won't I, sir!" Richard responded. "After all, you never know!"

"You never do, Richard!" replied Mr James winking a green, sparkly eye. "Books can sometimes surprise us!"

"This one certainly surprised me!" Richard replied, thoughtfully, turning to go out of the classroom and join his friends on the playground.

Would it have surprised Mr James, do you think?

I wonder!

# The End

Yes, this time it really is ......
....... or is it?

You'll just have to wait and see!

24559496R00087

Printed in Great Britain
by Amazon